ANCHORED
by
DEATH

A Jo Oliver Thriller
Book Three

Cover Design: Bookfly Design LLC.
Interior Design: Melinda Martin
Editor: Deb Haggerty

PUBLISHED BY: Elk Lake Publishing, Inc., 35 Dogwood Dr., Plymouth, MA 02360

Library Cataloging Data
Names: Finger Catherine (Catherine Finger)
Anchored by Death, Catherine Finger
240 p. 23cm × 15cm (9in × 6 in.)
Description: Elk Lake Publishing, Inc. digital e-book edition | Elk Lake Publishing, Inc. POD paperback edition | Elk Lake Publishing, Inc. 2017.
Identifiers: ISBN-13: 978-1-946638-10-6 (e-book) | 978-1-946638-11-3 (POD)
Key Words: Jo Oliver, murder, mystery, Christian, serial killer, romance, relationships
508746173405152017 F

ANCHORED
by
DEATH

A Jo Oliver Thriller
Book Three

Catherine Finger

Elk Lake
PUBLISHING, INC.

Plymouth, Massachusetts

PRAISE FOR CATHERINE FINGER'S

CLEANSED BY DEATH

"This skillfully crafted suspense story of a police chief tracking a serial killer will have you on the edge of your seat. Readers will root for Josie as she struggles to do the right thing, not only in her relationships but as she searches for answers about God. Catherine Finger has crafted a feisty heroine in Chief Josie Oliver as well as a cast of fascinating support characters. Looking forward to Catherine's next book in the series."

—**Patricia Bradley,** award-winning author of
Shadows of the Past

"Move over Kinsey Malone, Josie is in the house! This police chief is not only a local leader but respected throughout her community of coworkers, friends and good neighbors. She manages to overcome personal challenges while still putting the bad guy behind bars and reconciling her relationship with 'the magnificent being.'"

—**Elizabeth Martin Stearns,** Waukegan Public Library

"As a pastor, I rarely see characters in books or on screen who wrestle with God in a way that feels like what I see every day. *Cleansed by Death* is the rare exception, a world where spirituality is real but not easy, where the tragedies and triumphs of life work together to form a cohesive whole. I recommend it to anyone who has wrestled with God ... and loves a good mystery!"

—**Gary Ricci**, Pastor of New Hope Christian Community Church in Round Lake Heights, IL

"This Glock-toting, heel-wearing, justice-driven heroine in *Cleansed by Death* had me from the start. Unrelenting action and witty dialog kept me loving this ride-along until the very last page. A must-read."

—**Joseph Sugarman**, Chairman of Blublocker Sunglass Corporation

"In *Shattered by Death*, Catherine Finger takes us on a page-turning tale that keeps us riveted from beginning to end. With a crisp, clean writing style, Finger has crafted characters that stay with us long after we've finished the book. I can't wait for another release from this stellar author, who has just joined my favorite writers' list."

—**Kathi Macias**, author of more than fifty books, including Golden Scrolls 2011 Novel of the Year, *Red Ink*.

"Coming from a law-enforcement family, I especially enjoyed *Shattered by Death*. But anyone and everyone would love this intense, suspenseful novel that pulls you in from the very beginning and keeps you enthralled until the last word. I'm so glad this is part of a series. I'm hooked!"

—**Kathy Collard Miller**, speaker and author of many books including *Never Ever Be the Same*

PRAISE FOR CATHERINE FINGER'S

ANCHORED BY DEATH

"Catherine Finger has done it again. In this next installment of the Jo Oliver Thriller series, *Anchored by Death*, Finger paints a picture so vivid, so real, you won't believe you're not in the Midwest. The issues Jo Oliver must face are raw and real, but not too much for a great God to overcome. Hang onto your seat and enjoy the read!"

—**Toni Shiloh**, author of *Buying Love*

"Author Catherine Finger at her best. In book three of the *Jo Oliver Thriller* series, Police Chief Josie Oliver walks onto a golf course for some badly needed R&R and enters the twisted world of a serial killer. A murder investigation that forces her to confront her insecurities when she's reunited with the man she loves. *Anchored by Death* has all the twists and turns you've come to expect from this superb writer."

—**William Nikkel**, Amazon bestselling author of the *Jack Ferrell Adventure* series

"In Catherine Finger's latest installment in the Jo Oliver Thriller series, a string of murders in Wisconsin involving victims from Illinois at first suggests some sort of "redneck rivalry," but to readers' delight, ends up being so much more. Faithful, funny, and fearless, Josie tackles the mess that is her personal life with the same no nonsense approach she brings to her work as Police Chief. She bakes a flourless chocolate cake in the morning, tracks a murderer in the afternoon, and mends a broken relationship in the evening. All in a day's work for Finger's straight-shooting heroine."

--**Kelly Oliver**, Award-winning author of
The Jessica James Mysteries

"A great 5-star read. So good, I read it in two sittings."

--**Randy Tramp**, voracious reader,
frequent blogger, avid book reviewer

"An awesome thriller! Finger kept me guessing 'til the end. Loved the characters—they seem so real."

--**Wilani Wahi**, book lover, prolific reviewer

DEDICATION PAGE

To my beloved Wisconsin—
and the women and men who love her as much as I do.

Anchored by Death

ACKNOWLEDGMENTS

Just as the power of community is a central theme running through the Jo Oliver Thriller series, *Anchored by Death* celebrates the beauty of friendships old and new. I am graced with a strong circle of friends and dear family members who inspire me daily. Each and every one of them enriches my life and empowers my writing—thank you.

The writing process is a lonely journey. I am grateful for my partners old and new. The amazing Erynn Newman loves Josie almost as much as I do and improves my work with her thoughtful feedback and edits. Many thanks to my new friend and publishing partner, Deb Haggerty of Elk Lake Publishing, for believing in my work, loving my writing, and sharing her joy of living.

Faithful readers old and new—thank you for continually asking for the next story! I so enjoy getting to know you. Please continue reaching out and sharing your thoughts, ideas and reactions with me. Thank you for joining me on this wild ride of writing and storytelling.

"It's how you live that really counts."

—*Katharine Hepburn*

Anchored by Death

PROLOGUE

The feline in front of me grinned, stretching once-manicured claws one by one, green eyes boring into mine as if they held the key to life itself—or to the padded cuffs tethering her ankles and wrists to the table. "How's Nick? Been asking about me I suppose."

I tightened my lips, keeping an angry puff of air from escaping. "What do you want, Kira?"

She gave a slight shake of her head, sending a small shiver over dull brown hair. "Never one to beat around the bush."

I waited.

"Don't you just want to know why, Chiefy?" Her eyes narrowed into slits. *Like a snake.*

Why had the former police psychologist gone on a murder spree that nearly included my mother and me? No answer could really satisfy that question.

"Well, why not? Why the heck not? Haven't you ever had your fill of idiots and miscreants?" Her voice was half snarl, half seductress's whisper.

I blinked at her. *Where is she going now?*

"You think I enjoyed listening to them prattling on and on about perceived indignities and self-aggrandizement? You have no idea how torturous it can be. Can you even imagine being stuck in a room with one of them, alone, for fifty impossibly long minutes?" She shuddered.

"That was your job." I felt myself being pulled into the vortex of her crazy-making worldview. "That was what you *did.*"

"Until Nick came along." She stretched her neck toward me, clearly still hungry for the man I loved. "And everything changed." Images of the two of them together flashed through my mind. "He inspired me to greatness in one arena, and I transferred it to greatness in another."

Darkness crept up around me, tugging me down toward the swirling mouth of a rabbit hole full of self-hatred and regret. Paralysis gripped me, stole my voice.

"I watched him walk away from you when you pushed him away." She laughed. "Your stupidity made it all the easier—"

"For me to gut you like the animal you are." That terrible night came back to me in a rush. Nick's Leatherman clenched in my fist, my luring her close enough for me to deliver the blow that would stop her. In my mind's eye, I saw myself stabbing her, the hypodermic needle she held clattering to the hospital floor. "Not quite the happy ending you were hoping for though, was it, Kira?"

Her eyes glittered. "Happy enough. Unlike yours."

I looked away.

"Where's Nick now?" Kira leaned over the table and lowered her voice. "Have you brought that precious little girl home yet? Attempted murder put a little cramp in the paperwork filings?"

I stood up and slapped the table, aware of the purse by my feet and the crumpled letter inside, the gut-punching notice I'd found in the mailbox not two hours ago. *Pending an investigation ... your application to adopt has been put on hold.*

"What do you know about that?"

She withdrew, grinning. "Idiots and miscreants. Which one are you?"

I sucked in a lungful of the fetid air and let it out, scrolling through the numbers one to ten in my mind, angry with myself for being baited into talking about my daughter with this monster.

"Enjoy your vacation, Chief." Her steely tone couldn't mask the sliver of desperation in her eyes.

I looked up at the camera over her head and gave two sharp nods. *Come and get me.*

It was time to go home.

CHAPTER ONE

Samantha's hair shimmered with the blues and reds that sparked off the screen. Her feet were lodged against mine as we stood together in the classic shooter stance before my mother's small television. A better woman would have spent our last day together in church—maybe followed by a Sunday-school picnic. After all, at the end of this glorious weekend together, my daughter and I would be apart for a week. But hearing Sammie's laughter, watching her face light up as we faced a horde of zombies together convinced me I'd made the right choice.

"On your left!" my aging mom warned from her wheelchair beside the sofa.

Samantha's little shoulders shook and turned with her as she mowed down one group of zombies after another. A monster was hiding behind a rock on the far edge of the screen. I knelt beside my daughter, wireless remote in hand, and shot it right between the eyes the minute it peered over at her little blonde warrior avatar.

"Good one, Mama!" Sammie's voice was honey over buttered chocolate-chip pancakes.

Zombies froze in place before us as I set the controller down, wrapped my arms around her and kissed her head. "I love you, little warrior of mine."

"If we ever have a zombie invasion, I know who to call," my mother said in her thready but cheerful voice.

Sammie bolted to my mother's side, ignoring her wheelchair and scrambling up onto her lap. "I drew some pictures for you."

"Pictures of a zombie apocalypse?"

Samantha giggled. "No! Of us playing games!" My mother kissed my daughter-to-be, looked up at me and winked. "So where are they?"

My mother always knew exactly what to say. Where did she get that stuff? *Will I know the right things to say to Samantha when I'm on my own?*

"Mama! Where's Grandma's art?" Sam glared the question at me.

"I'll go get it." Sometimes obedience was the only answer.

"Yes, do. We girls need a little time alone together, don't we, Samantha?" My mother dismissed me with another wink and a smile.

I walked out into the corridor of my mother's independent-living community. The fresh-paint, fresh-plaster smell was almost overwhelming. The transformation of this place from a burned-out shell into a beautiful new wing was nothing short of a miracle. Kira's long, vengeful arm had nearly destroyed everything, everyone I cared most about. A wave of nausea rolled over me, and I leaned into the freshly papered wall for support.

Much as I tried to pretend, I really wasn't okay. My own scars were fading, the bad girl was behind bars, and the damaging effects of her terror were lessening every day. Still, I wasn't anywhere near ready for full-time motherhood. But, the fact that the chance might be taken away brought out the fighter in me.

I fetched the pictures from the car and returned to the room to find Samantha and Mom seated at her table, happily chatting, engrossed in a game of cribbage. Or something like cribbage. I squeezed their shoulders as Mom admired Sammie's art, then

I posted the masterpieces on the fridge before sitting down to soak in the scene.

An hour later, I broke the news it was time to take Samantha back to her foster family. *Hopefully, for one of the last times.*

"But, Mama!" As she came to me, I saw the softness in her eyes melt away, revealing the fear that still simmered just under the surface. "Let me go home with you. *Please.* I only want to stay with *you!*"

I pulled her into my body, wishing I could shield her, warm her heart, whisk away the memories of her own lost parents, the ever-present fear of losing me too. *Lord God, please replace her fear with Your love.* I glanced at my mom, who smiled at me as she put away the game. I hadn't told her about the adoption letter.

"You *will* be with me forever, Samantha, very soon. But for a little while yet, we need to let you stay with your current family. They love you very much, and they need time to say good-bye to you."

"Is it because you have to go?"

"Boss's orders." Therapist's orders, actually, for some R and R away from the pull of my job with the Haversport Police Department. He wasn't ready to clear me for full-time work just yet. "I'll be back in next weekend. You'll be so busy with school and your friends, the time will fly!" I loosened my grip and made kissing noises. "It's time for a kiss attack!" I tickled her and loudly and kissed her head, her face, her arms, anything within kissing distance as she shrieked and danced and laughed.

Her laughter soothed my spirit. Anything to pull her away from the dangers of the past and back into my arms, back into her present and toward our beautiful future together. "Darling girl—"

"Don't you mean warrior daughter?"

"Darling warrior daughter of mine." More kisses, more squeals. "I love you so much. And you have so many people in your life who love you as much as I do."

"But you already are my forever mama, aren't you?" Hope gleamed where sorrow had been a few seconds ago.

I knelt before her, willing my own tears away. *Anything to wipe it all away.* "Yes. I. Am. Your. Forever. Mama. Now. And I love you. I love you. I love you. I lov—"

"Ew! I got it. I got it, Mama! Now sto-op!" Her little girl shrug and eye roll nearly threw me over the edge into laughter, but I held it in. "Mama, can I ask you something?" Blue eyes shimmered up at me.

"Of course, baby."

"I'm not a baby!"

"Of course not, baby." I winked at her.

"Mama, where's Nick? Isn't he my forever Nick too?"

Ice-cold water hit my veins. *Nick. Again?* Mom caught my eye and shook her head. How long could I protect Samantha from his absence? It wasn't for me to say when he'd come back. If he ever came back.

"Sammie, Nick is off on a mission. He loves you—he loves us both, but he's off on a mission." *That ought to satisfy her. For now.*

She sighed and nodded.

"Besides, in just a few days, I will come right back to you and scoop you back up into my arms."

She smiled. "And that's where I'm staying, Mama. Forever in your arms." She threw her long limbs around my neck.

I choked back tears, wanting her to hear and feel only warmth and happiness for the rest of today. "Yes, baby. Forever in my arms."

CHAPTER TWO

The wind swept through the pine trees drooping over the glossy fairway. I closed my eyes and breathed deeply, my lucky seven iron anchoring my right side. The scent of pine needles mixed with damp earth freshened my soul, and I opened my eyes to hunt for my little white foe. I'd already scoured the tall grass hugging the right of the fairway, giving a wide berth to the roped-off area that snaked between two large maple trees in the middle of the fairway.

Indian burial mounds were scattered throughout the Baraboo region of Wisconsin, and those of us from around these parts had been raised to respect the living and the dead—of all races, colors, and creeds. I really didn't like to enter the sacred ground, but I also didn't like the idea of leaving another white ball lying around on top of the ancient dead. Seemed disrespectful. Especially since this ball had my initials engraved on it.

Still sentimental. I ducked under the woven yellow rope and gingerly stepped onto the edge of the mound. The ground had yet to thaw completely so I wouldn't have to worry about leaving footprints behind. The mound sloped gently upward to a height of maybe four feet in the middle, flowing back down into the shape of a thunderbird, covering about two hundred square feet. There were three separate burial mounds on this hole alone, five all told on the course. Each one symbolized an important Native American deity.

I stepped back, trying to remember which mound of dirt represented the wingspan and which the profiled head and beak. A small stump jutted out of the ground near what I thought was the head of the bird. Odd. I'd never seen it before. No way could a tree have grown and died in just one season. I'd played golf here last fall, and the mound had been pristine.

The wind shifted directions, sending a whistling through the pines. I scanned the area, noting I was still the only person visible on the course. Typical early spring day in Wisconsin. No one would be on the golf course at this hour—especially since you could still see your breath before noon. I'd gone to high school with the club owner, and he was fine with me sneaking onto the course, as long as I let him know ahead of time. Which I would do, as soon as I finished playing. I liked my me-time.

A chill inched up my spine. I shook off the feeling and returned my attention to the stump, golf ball chase momentarily forgotten. Was it even a stump? What else could the thing be? It jutted up from the earth a foot, maybe a foot and a half, and looked for all the world like a dark, capped mushroom. I gripped my lucky seven iron and took a few steps forward.

The wind picked up again, and the mushroom's cap jiggled for an instant, stopping me in my tracks. *What the ...? Can't be a stump, can it?*

I had involuntarily raised my iron as if to ward off an intruder. My senses were on high alert. I patted the shoulder holster under my windbreaker, relieved to feel the comforting presence of my off-duty Glock. *Calm down, girl! Breathe.*

The wind picked up speed, jostling the top of the stump again, then suddenly changed directions. The rush of wind slapped my face, stinging my eyes, and I put my arm up to shield them.

But not before I watched what looked like a French beret fly up off of the tree stump in a macabre dance on the gusty spring air.

The beret floated over a stand of scrub trees, fluttering above them for a few seconds before landing in scraggly branches. I walked over and stuck out my lucky seven iron, hooking the cap. A tattered brown ribbon edged the bottom of it. An English brand, featuring a fox-and-hound motif, was stamped onto the faded tag inside. A smaller square tag belted my first real clue—a logo from the International Spy Museum.

The cop in me surfaced. I tugged down on my golf glove and stuffed the cap into my back pocket. If some knucklehead had been out here intentionally desecrating the effigy mounds, this might lead to him. Or her. Couldn't I enjoy a lousy round of golf without the specter of crime shadowing my every move? Heck, here I was, hours from Haversport, thinking about a possible hate crime. Ah, probably just some city boy's lost lid. End of story.

I took a deep breath and gasped. My cracked ribs hadn't gone on holiday just because I was on vacation. The flash of pain brought back fiery snippets of scenes I'd rather not remember. Nick's love stamped all over his handsome face, hazy in my mind, faded away behind an imposing vision of Kira, hypodermic needle in hand, intent to kill burning in her eyes as she loomed over my hospital bed. Only her evil plans hadn't worked out that way. Neither Nick nor Kira got what they came for that fateful day.

Two months later, Kira was behind bars, still causing me trouble, Nick was MIA, and I'd gone back to work as soon as the docs reluctantly released me from the hospital. I figured returning to my routine might help nurse my wounded heart while my body slowly came back to life. Fat chance.

Samantha. Her name floated through my mind. I closed my eyes, offering up quick prayers for her protection and joy. I opened my eyes and touched the cap in my back pocket. Was my vacation about to come to an abrupt halt before it even began? I hoped not. I still had some sorting out to do.

I shook my head, pushing those thoughts away. Then I turned and made my way back to the burial mound. The topless mushroom had morphed into something very different now that I had a man's cap in my pocket. Vibrations of dread seemed to radiate from the lump in the ground. Fear shuddered through me with each step. I focused on the hatless thing until I had to shift from thinking of it as an "it" and into a gruesome new reality. *Rats. I am not in the mood for this kind of reality.*

All I'd really wanted was some peace and quiet. An opportunity to move past my average eighty-yard drive into maybe something closer to ninety. I wasn't asking for the moon. I never expected to win the County Cops Open—I just wanted to show up and not wish I was driving the cart instead of my Cobra for once.

I pushed my aspirations aside and forced myself to think like the cop I was. Holy cats. I had a guy's cap in my pocket. And I was almost certain the beret belonged on the "stump" that was sticking up out of the Indian burial mound on the sixth green of the Baraboo Country Club Golf Course.

Reaching the edge of the mound, I squatted down on my heels, not quite ready to view the front of what was clearly a human head. The unmistakable smell of death wafted up around the not-stump. Dark hair was plastered in gloomy hanks on the back. Pulling out my phone, I snapped a few dozen photos from all conceivable angles before my curiosity surfaced anew.

I used the club to push myself to my feet. My knees were shaking. I bent at the waist and took a deep, measured breath, regretting breathing the minute the smell hit my olfactory sensors. After several seconds had passed, I rose slowly and stepped around the rope to the center of the effigy mound, making my way to the front of the head. Heavily jowled, lids mercifully closed, the man's face was quiet in death. Which meant absolutely nothing. There's no way he'd have just decided to take what my aunt Gerry would have called "a dirt nap" on the sixth green and died peacefully while up to his neck in a hole in the ground.

The earth was a river of striated gullies, the mud thick and layered. There were no telltale prints leading off in one direction or another. Stepping away from the body, I scanned the course. *Why did you choose this hole?* The fairway stood at the bottom of a steep hill on one side, a river rushing down a ravine on another. *You scoped this out, chose this spot with care. But why?*

I looked around at the varied heights of the scrub and fruit trees bordering the other two sides. Whoever had buried this man knew his way around this fairway. From the looks of this burial site, he also knew his geology.

I carefully put my iron down on the grass and bowed my head. What happened to a man's soul when he died? Did it go straight to one gate or the other? Did the soul go to some kind of cosmic holding tank? I was too new at the game as a believer to have any idea.

I decided to file the question away and ask a certain gorgeous Cuban security consultant to tell me all the ins and outs. Gino Rivera had been my spiritual mentor and part-time protector ever since we met at a crime scene nearly a decade ago. Back when he was still a cop.

Lately though, since my stellar decision to break things off with Nick, Gino had been more full-time than a part-time guide. According to him, between my poorly managed personal life and my natural ability to find trouble, I needed both men on duty around the clock just to keep me breathing.

Over the years, he'd been proven right on several occasions. For a long time, we'd been inseparable. Nick Vitarello (my hot Italian boyfriend and nationally acclaimed FBI agent), Gino, and me—the top cop of a small town police force with a big-city solve rate. My department's rep for getting the job done right had earned us nonstop invitations to assist our boys in blue in neighboring communities. Our resources were stretched so thin, I'd already developed the habit of sending out investigators alone to complex cases—against my best judgment—but I just didn't have the manpower to keep up with the crime. With Nick and Gino by my side, though, I'd always been able to cope. I'd come to think of them as my guardian angels. We'd been known as the Triumvirate for years. What did that make us now?

I took a second to ground myself. I needed to call Sheriff Tom Quinn. I sighed. Facing an old childhood friend and a dead body on an empty stomach was above my pay grade. Gino and I had planned a catch-up call once I got off the links, but that would have to wait. I pulled out my phone and tapped Gino's handsome face, red do-rag artfully wrapped around his head. I frowned as his voice mail came on. Good old Wisconsin. Nine months of winter, three months of poor sledding, and absolutely lousy cell phone reception. I left Gino a message letting him know I'd call as soon as I reported "an incident" to the local boys. *First things first.* I ended the call and scrolled through the other faces on my iPhone.

The photo I used for my old pal Sheriff Tom Quinn was straight off his web page. I knew his personal number by heart, but for the life of me, I could not find his official number listed anywhere. I could have looked a little harder. Instead, I pressed the face of the sweet guy I'd gone to high school with back in the day.

"Mornin', Sheriff Quinn." I paused, giving him time to recognize my voice.

"Josie, is that you?" There was a boyish delight in his voice that made me smile.

Memories of perfect winter evenings spent necking before a roaring fire in his cabin in the woods, of sharing our dreams and fears while snuggling in deer blinds hours on end sifted through my mind. I closed my eyes, breathing them in, sitting with the memories before breaking the spell. "Yes, it is, Sheriff. And this isn't a social call."

CHAPTER THREE

Sheriff Quinn was a man of few words. Just like every other guy I'd grown up with. When he said, "See you in ten," right before ending the call, I knew he must've been having coffee in town. I slid on my favorite pair of BluBlockers and stood up to scan the area.

Crisp morning air breezed across my face, and I thought of a picture in my bedroom. White sailboat dancing on the waves, the words "Trust that the wind knows where it's going," painted against the windswept dark blue sky. It always made me think of the way the Holy Spirit worked in my life, pulling me into His leading if only I would just take my hand off the helm and let Him steer. *Big if. And not my strong suit.* Over the years, I'd grown rather fond of being a one-woman show.

I was just learning how to give up control of my life to God as I understood Him. Foreign territory. So far, all I had going for me in that department was a few Bible verses I had memorized but didn't exactly understand. Like this one from James 4:7. *Submit therefore to God. Resist the devil, and he will flee from you.*

What did that have to do with the DB? I sighed. What the heck? Couldn't hurt. *Father, please forgive me for trying to run things, and help me submit to You in every way. And I rebuke the devil and any spirit of confusion surrounding this man—this case. I commit it all to You.*

Gino'd be proud. Prayer was coming more naturally to me, just like he'd promised. The crunch of tires on gravel pulled my gaze up the hill. A Sauk County Sheriff's squad car was making its way to me.

Tom Quinn was at the wheel. His head nearly touched the squad's ceiling, and he looked a little gaunt. He stopped the car beside the burial mound, sunglasses shielding his reaction to seeing me again. He sat a moment longer, gave a slight shake of his head and slid out unfolding his six-foot-five-inch frame. He stepped in front of the dead body or DB in police lingo and removed a small roll of perimeter tape from one pocket and a pair of gloves from another.

He pulled on the gloves and withdrew a camera from his shirt pocket. Economy in motion. And still no words.

"He ain't fresh." Quinn examined the head, snapped a finger against the skull.

"Nope."

"You call this into one of your big-shot boyfriends?" He took several pictures of the head.

"Nope. Your jurisdiction." I was sucking up. A little.

He froze at that, pulled back a little, almost looking up. But then, he thought better of it and leaned into the gruesome scene, resuming his photography.

"You touch the body anywhere?"

I shook my head.

His brows scowled at me. "Suppose you just had to get involved. Couldn't hold your horses and wait for me, huh?" He'd learned about my impulsive behavior firsthand. But that was then. This was now.

"Nope. Thought about it though. Prayed and decided to wait." It just slipped out.

"No kiddin'?" He pursed his lips, eyebrows raised and looked up at me.

Had I finally impressed him?

Quinn eyed me like a butcher appraising a tenderloin. "You *prayed* about it? Well, now that's differ'nt. Learn anything off it? Them prayers, I mean?" He squatted back on his haunches, bespectacled gaze fixed on me. I think.

"Just to call you in. So, I did." *If you tell a little white lie about praying, is it still a lie?* Why was I trying so hard to clue him in to my newfound spirituality? Why was I sidling up to him? Just being here on this course with him seemed to erase the years between us. I was all eager girl matching his country boy code, word for silent pause.

"That what did it?" He squinted, squeezing his brows together.

"Yup. Well, the part about it being smack in the middle of your jurisdiction didn't hurt. But I did toss one up to the Almighty. Proud of me? But anyway, this isn't about us. This is about him." I nodded my head at the man in the mound.

"Yup. Mostly." He reddened. A slip of the tongue? "Josie, there's a lot more going on here than meets the eye. Let's review the evidence between us—"

"Tom, give me a minute." I decided to head this off at the pass. "Look, I'm sorry I've been such a nonexistent jerk. I abandoned my Wisconsin roots, ran off to Illinois and didn't say good-bye. There's nothing I can say that's going to ever make that okay. And I couldn't be sorrier about all of it. More than you'll ever know." I was already saying more than I'd intended.

"Ain't you leaving out some pretty big chunks?" Pain seeped out of his voice.

"Quinn, let's ... not ..." I didn't want to go there with him. I was sick of talking about it already, and we hadn't even started.

"The part about you living through a wall of nonstop pain and me not being there for you? About me being the worst friend this side of the Kickapoo River?" He'd ditched his country boy, aw-shucks style. I'd forgotten how quickly his hick accent could fade away.

"My lousy marriage was not your ..." I didn't know where I was going with this—where I wanted to go.

Hunger noises wrangled up from my belly loud enough for him to hear. Flames of embarrassment shot through my cheeks.

He stood up, laughing. "Not to worry. I got you covered." He fished around in his jacket pocket, making lots of crinkling noises and brought his hand out in a fist. He turned his hand over and reached out to me. "Peace?"

I burst out laughing, grabbing my sides. "Peace." I accepted his offering, then wrapped my arms around him.

We stood there on the golf course hugging for several seconds. Then, I pulled away from him and looked down at the bag of BBQ Corn Nuts, which started a fresh wave of laughter.

Quinn stepped away from me and called it in, requesting backup and crime-scene techs. I tore open the bag and slipped a small handful of the salty-sweet corn snacks into my mouth.

The DB wasn't dressed like anyone from around here, but something about his features rang a distant bell in my head. I'm sure Quinn would've noticed the-out-of-towner apparel. No doubt he'd be calling for a vehicle check, looking for out-of-town plates, maybe out-of-state even.

He did his sheriff thing with crisp efficiency. Gone was the awkward dance of the junior high Quinn. He was on his throne, even in the middle of a golf course. Past him on the velvety fairway, a cardinal cawed and pecked on a pin oak lining the rough. How would today's horrible discovery impact this little universe? Would the course open on time? Would they keep this hole in play, or would they leave the effigy mound and microscopic remnants of its newest resident to rest in peace for a season?

It was impossible to predict the impact of a violent death on lives left behind. I'd seen it all—anger channeled into positive action, lives stagnating in the numbness of perpetual depression, people succumbing to a life of restless abandon.

Yes, I'd seen my share of crime and had a seat at the table of the people left behind. Yet, out of all the crime scenes I'd had the extreme displeasure to attend in the past several years, I'd never seen this. At least his calm features suggested he'd been dead before the burial.

Or so I hoped.

CHAPTER FOUR

The crime-scene techs swarmed the mound, recording every detail. From the sounds of it, this was their first golf course vic. Way too many lame golf jokes wafted over from a sparky group of techs detailing the area. Definitely old school—they'd formed a square around the victim with field cord. I knew from my own time in the saddle as a crime-scene tech the next few hours would be spent examining every square inch within the cordoned-off area.

I also knew several of those square inches would be pretty well contaminated by now. While I never found the errant Mojo brand golf ball that had brought me to this ancient Indian burial site, I sure had stomped all over the mound before realizing I was looking right at a DB. What did that say about my state of mind? Maybe I needed a little more time off.

"Don't be so hard on yourself, Jo. If it'd been easy to see, the body would've been found before now." Quinn was at my side, answering my thoughts as if reading my mind. I hadn't even noticed his approach. I really *was* off my game.

"Yeah. How long do you think he's been out here?" No doubt, Quinn was still keeping tabs on his town. He'd never let that slide. Not the way we'd let each other slide away all those years ago.

Quinn narrowed his eyes and looked at me. "Longer than either of us would like, from the smell of things, I reckon. Poor man's been out here by his lonesome for a while now." His inner hick was out again, but this time it had a sharp undertone. Something else entirely was on his mind.

I arched an eyebrow and turned to stare at him. "What's going on, Quinn?"

"I'm hoping there's no connection ..." His voice was low and slow. "And you've clearly established this is not the time to get into history, ancient or otherwise. Josie, there's something I've got to tell—" A red-hot flash of ... anger? Desire? *Something* sparked in his eyes, vanishing almost before it registered. *Almost.* "There'll be time for that later."

But, the flush spreading across my face and my dancing belly verified what I'd just seen. My eyes searched his grizzled face, locking onto his liquid chocolate browns. I tried to pull my gaze away but found myself drawn to him. I steadied myself, found the tiny white speck in his left eye and drank him in.

He stepped nearer, standing so close that if I bent my knees, they would brush up against his. I locked my legs in place, willed my arms to relax at my sides and drew in a deep breath. My mind swirled at his scent. He brought back memories of wild midnight horseback rides under snow-dipped pines, Wisconsin River sandbars, and long moments kissing under a perfect harvest moon, knee deep in the autumn splendor of Devil's Lake.

He locked eyes with me, and for a moment, I fell back in time. I took two steps back, my only defense against the solid comfort he evoked. We stood looking at each other. *He's trying to tell me something.*

"Look, but don't touch. Is that it?" He grinned.

"Something like that." I snorted.

"You're still in love with Nick, aren't you?" His grin faded.

"Something like that," I admitted as much to myself as to Quinn. I could see he had something else on his mind, but I couldn't get past the dance.

Quinn appraised me, ardor that had threatened to swallow me whole seconds ago nowhere to be found. "Figures."

Talk about your sudden gust of cold air.

"Yup." I had no idea why I was yupping.

"Got something, boss. And it looks way too familiar." A chipper squeak from one of his newbies drew Quinn's attention from me.

I shot a glance upward, breathing a quick prayer. *Thank You.*

Quinn waited for me to join him. We strode over to the crime-scene tech. Her heart-shaped face glanced up at us from her perch on the ground in front of the victim. She was lovely, dark, and petite. The polar opposite of me. I turned to Quinn. *What's a girl like that doing in a place like this?* He shrugged.

"We're not completely backward around here, you know. We still take our girls seriously," he whispered, nudging past me to join her.

"Check it out, Sheriff. Tell me you haven't seen this type of thing before." She squatted back on her heels, making room for Quinn. Her name tag read Lisa Bhatt. I focused my attention on her more intently. Her skin glowed with olive and brown tones, a splash of cream thrown in. Her eyes were almond shaped, with the kind of lashes most women have to buy. She wasn't wearing a speck of makeup, making her all the more extraordinary.

She looked up at me, patient with my scrutiny. "Chief Oliver. I've waited for my entire career to meet you." She unfolded, gracefully rising to meet me.

My knees cracked just watching her. *Time to get back into the yoga studio.*

"Lisa Bhatt." Her accent was slight, musical. She stuck out a slim brown hand, delicate fingers clenching my own with sufficient force.

Color me impressed. "Where are you from, Officer Bhatt?"

"Lisa. Please call me Lisa. I'm from Ohio. Cleveland area." Amusement wrinkled the corners of her eyes.

Of course she is. Good one, Josie. You're making a heckuva fool of yourself without even trying. "Well, I'm from here. Nice to meet you." Not my cleverest response. "What have you got?"

She was too well-bred to acknowledge my discomfort. "This doesn't seem to fit here, does it?" She pointed with her field knife to a small white object on the ground. The knife marks around it confirmed she'd scratched it up out of the earth. "We just started to explore the soil around the DB, thinking of how best to excavate. I felt something against my blade."

"You felt that?" I nodded my head at the white square. "With *that*?" I pointed to her knife, admiration dripping from my every word.

She blushed. "Yeah. I guess." A shy smile blossomed.

"Good work. Great attention to detail." I pursed my lips. "But what is it? Looks almost like a fat Scrabble tile. Is that an *H* printed on it?"

She nodded enthusiastically. "Yeah. That's what I thought too. Until I saw this." She picked up the tiny square block with a gloved hand. "It's a hole. All the way through. It's a bead."

"As in from a necklace?" I tried to picture a necklace made of square block letters.

"Or a bracelet." Quinn was still in the game. He exchanged glances with Bhatt, a team of two.

"I was thinking more like ankle bracelet, but yes, it's definitely a bead of some sort." She gave a slight shrug as if she found clues that her colleagues missed at crime scenes every day.

"Doesn't strike me as a Scrabble-jewelry kind of guy." I had a wearying knack for stating the obvious.

"And yet, here it is. Just like the last vic—" Bhatt inhaled sharply, eyes fixed on Quinn.

I caught a slight shake of his head as he shot a look from Bhatt to the ground and back to me.

"Fine, keep your secrets." I closed my eyes, kneading the soft flesh over my temples in a desperate attempt to stop a migraine before it got started. *Relax.* Another reason I needed this vacation.

At this rate, I was going to need a little time off *from* my vacation.

"We can take it from here, Josie. You want me to take you home?" Quinn's eyes twinkled.

Officer Bhatt shook her head, smiled and threw him a wry glance. "Alrighty then. You kids have fun. Call if you're going to be out all night, 'kay, boss?"

Quinn scowled at her. "I'll be back in half an hour. Any other clues come up while I'm gone, give me a shout, got it?" He waited for her quick nod before turning to me.

"C'mon, Josie. I'll drive." Nodding toward my abandoned golf cart, he winked at me and started walking toward the driver's side.

I waved at Lisa Bhatt and scrambled after him. "Hey, *boss.* Give me a sec while I put away my not-so-lucky seven iron and cover up my clubs. Since you're clearly not up to the job."

Bhatt's laughter jingled on the wind behind me. "He's not much of a golfer, Chief. And he definitely likes to be in the driver's seat. But, I'll place my money on you."

Quinn's coded language with Bhatt told me they wanted their privacy. Something else was going on related to this case—something they wanted to keep to themselves for now. Whatever it was, I'd leave them to it awhile longer. "Smart girl you've got there, pal. Where'd you find her?" I jumped into the cart.

He pushed the accelerator and wheeled the cart around, steering us toward a line of trees behind the longer wing of the earthen thunderbird. "I didn't. She found us. Don't ask me why she wanted to work with the original hickstone cops, 'cause I have no idea. She's a good CSI with excellent instincts. And she's about to become an even better detective." We wove between the trees and headed up a steep incline.

"She must have a pretty thick skin to make it through training with the redneck knuckleheads she no doubt encountered." I thought back to my own training days in Chicago and shivered.

"You paved the way for her." Quinn's quiet reverence endeared him to me.

"Aw, thank you." I squeezed his shoulder, then grabbed the hand bar as the cart rocked over the uneven hillside terrain. We ducked in unison as the cart top swooshed under a low-hanging branch, laughing at the sound of leaves scratching across the black plastic top.

We broke out of the trees onto the neatly mowed turf leading from the golf course to the edge of the property I'd inherited from my aunt years ago.

"Whoa. Nice work, Josie." He seemed to be staring at the circular expanse of brick pavers I'd had installed around my fire pit last fall. The pavers narrowed to a path for about ten feet before gradually dwindling down to nothing. Another ten feet of earth led to a green electrical box jutting out of the ground. The rest of the lot was thick with trees.

Quinn maneuvered around the trees, up over the hill, spied my car parked in the street and headed toward it. "I take it you still haven't decided whether to build or sell?"

Forgot how small towns work. He knows my every move around here. "Pretty much. And you know how it is. Might as well make a few improvements while you're trying to decide, right?" I'd inherited this lot nearly twenty years ago, long before I was married. It was one of the few things in my life that had survived the deaths of both my marriage and my husband. His and his mistress's brutal murders seemed a lifetime past now, but they were really only a few months ago.

I'd lost so much more than my marriage in that whole grisly affair. By the end of the investigation, I'd nearly lost my own life … twice. *But hey, who's counting?* Worst of all, I'd lost Nick.

Quinn's voice mercifully ended my ruminating. "And your aunt Gerry would be rolling in her grave if she knew you'd built a fire pit like some poor relation, instead of the luxury home this lot requires." He pulled the cart up to the trunk of my car.

"I like to think she'd be smiling down on me for my eccentricities." We rolled to a stop. I popped my trunk, unstrapped my clubs and stood aside while Quinn placed them in the back.

He turned around to face me as I slammed the trunk shut. We stood looking at each other in the street, awkward teenagers alone in the science lab after school. He ran a hand through his hair.

I stepped in and lightly kissed him on the cheek. "Thanks, Quinn." I turned and stepped into my car, leaving him looking at me from the side of the road. He didn't move as I started my car, winked at him in the side mirror and slowly drove away.

CHAPTER FIVE

The car's console lit up a second before the cell phone's signature chirp filled my car. I smiled when I read the name. "Hey, Georgi." Breathing out my old friend's name loosened my neck muscles.

"I just heard. Where are you?" Georgi and I had been friends since meeting in the ninth grade. She married her high school sweetheart and never left the little town we'd all grown up in. Her connections were legendary. "You still on the course with Quinn?"

I rolled my eyes and smiled into the console. "No, just leaving. Quinn's got 'er under control. You hear about the vic? Buried up to his neck in a mound?" A sudden need to talk it out gripped me.

"Yeah, and about the wooden block with the letter *H* printed on it. What the heck could that mean?" If Georgi knew this much, this soon, the entire town would be in on the murder by now.

"Whoa, hold on. You wanna brainstorm? I'm happy to drop by." I didn't know what exactly she'd heard, but I wasn't comfortable spilling it over the unprotected airwaves for any amateur hack's amusement.

"I'll do you one better. Why don't you swing by and pick me up, and we can head out to your place? Go for a walk and then invite the boys to join us for dinner and a fire." She was rustling around and zippering a bag as she spoke.

"That'll work. I'll be there in five. Maybe three." Small town driving was just like flying. "Wait a minute. What do you mean 'invite the boys'? What boys?"

"I'm on the porch. And by the way, you're cooking. We're building the fire." She must've put her hand over the phone. Dodging my question? Her husband's garbled voice mixed with hers in the background as they negotiated details of the evening.

When I pulled up to her house a minute later, she and Cliff were sitting on the porch steps, her phone still in her hand, Cliff's arms around her waist. I ended the call and got out of the car.

Cliff whisked Georgi down the porch steps and wrapped me in his signature bear hug. "Good to see you, Chief. Sorry about that mess on the golf course. You girls have fun at the lake, and we'll be by in a few hours." He looked at me, hope swimming in his eyes.

"Don't go getting your hopes up. I'm thinking a simple meal of pasta and salad and all the beer you can drink. And I might have a few other items hanging around the cabin to round out our meal." I wasn't about to ask who *we* referred to. As far as Cliff was concerned, when it came to my love life, hope sprang eternally. He'd probably invited Quinn to dinner before I pulled up to the house.

"It wouldn't exactly be against the law for you to whip up your triple-chocolate cake, now would it?" Happiness sparked off him at the idea. "I'm pretty sure you-know-who would be putty in your hands after a bite or two of that cake. You could put him to work on those loose shingles and have him tack that gutter back in place once we leave." He held both hands palm up as if to show me he had nothing to hide.

"Hey, how's our little Samantha, and when will we see her again? Are you bringing her back up for the weekend?" Georgi must've remembered how much Sam also loved my triple-chocolate cake.

"She's amazing, and yes, that's exactly my plan. Or, I guess I should say it was my plan before encountering a DB today. And I think it's still the plan unless Quinn needs my help with our golfer."

"Good," Cliff said. "I can't wait to hug that little squirt. And take her fishing." He was a dear man with a soft heart. I nodded at him and looked over at Georgi. "You about ready to go?"

Georgi elbowed him in the ribs and gave him a quick kiss. "We'll call when we're ready. Probably around five or six." She grabbed my arm. "Ignore him. He wants everyone to be happy. Whatever that means."

"Yeah. Me too." We walked to my car in unison and got in without another word.

While I had a few guesses as to which of our lifelong friends Cliff might have in mind to bring tonight, I knew who wouldn't be coming to dinner.

Nick Vitarello stood like a Roman statue in the center of my mind and within a hair's breadth of my heart, but I had locked and bolted the door.

He'd stood by me as we tracked a vicious killer, fending off repeated attempts on my life and my constant rejection of his romantic overtures. The last time I saw him, I was in a hospital bed, loaded with painkillers. He was at my side when I woke up. Moments later, he declared his love for me. But he knew I was afraid, and rather than subject himself to more of my see-sawing heart, he took a giant step back. He'd pledged to wait for me to sort out my feelings and to come to him on my own terms.

But he hadn't said how long he'd wait. Or how I was supposed to signal him when I was ready. Was I ready? I wasn't sure. Still. So, I just stayed stuck, silent, and stoic on the outside, roiling with indecision and regret on the inside. I sighed. Nick was destined to remain a very present force in my heart and mind, but not in my life.

At least not yet. But things could change, right?

"Must've been pretty bad, huh?" Giorgi's whisper filled the car.

I nodded. "Never seen anything like it. And the funny thing is, I saw it without realizing what it was. I walked right past, registering it, wondering how I would've missed a stump on that hole before now." I rolled through the scene in my mind again, picturing the beret floating on the spring wind.

"What kind of freak would bury a guy in a sacred resting place? And what do you make of the letter *H*? That's gotta be a clue, right?" Her voice rose several octaves. She was all in.

I scrunched my nose and turned to stare at her. "The *H* almost has to be a clue. Though of what, I couldn't hazard a guess." I grunted. "I mean, what do we know? The vic was an insurance salesman from Illinois. Franklin Park."

"Or it could've been placed there as a clue." Her purse buzzed. She rummaged through it, found her phone and answered.

I recognized her mother's tinny voice on the other end. Their conversation kept Georgi engaged long enough for me to drive the rest of the way to my small cabin, deep in thought about what that single letter could mean.

I wondered if there was a connection between the wayward letter *H* and the victim's hometown. While I wasn't aware of any killers leaving clues of their victims' home address at a crime scene, I really wouldn't be shocked.

Could it be one of the killer's initials? A band of tension wrapped itself around my head. Or maybe it was the killer's calling card. The band snapped against my temples. Nick would know if there were other cases involving tiles, beads, or letters left at the crime scene. Too bad we were completely out of touch.

I knew from experience understanding the mind of a psychopath was impossible, let alone that of a random murderer. One of my first murder investigations involved a fourteen-year-old boy who had killed his cousin over an Atari game stick. Guy like that could eventually kill over bigger sticks if he didn't get caught. Could this whole thing be over a golf game?

"So, we have a guy from Illinois dead and buried on a patch of land in Wisconsin. Do you think this could have anything to do with the old Wisconsin-Illinois rivalry?" she asked, matter-of-factly, as if a rivalry murder happened every day.

I glanced at her. "You're kidding, right?"

"Well, you know stuff like that happens. And you know lots of guys around here can't stand guys from Illinois. Just sayin'." She twisted to face me on the seat.

"Don't you think that's a little over the top, Georgi?"

"Maybe, but it's pretty odd to have a guy from Illinois murdered on a golf course in Wisconsin. There's got to be a reason. What if it's that simple—what if it's just some crazed local who's got it out for anyone from the flatlands?"

"But *something* bothers you about this cold-blooded burial killing? That's actually a relief." I chuckled. "So, I give. What's bugging you?"

"Well, the whole scene bugs me. First off, out of all the golf courses in the Baraboo-Dells area, he chooses the Baraboo Country Club. That can't be a coincidence." She fished an envelope and a pen out of her purse and started to draw. "And he happens to select the sixth hole, which just happens to be the only hole on the only course in the area that boasts an ancient Indian burial mound as a feature. Again, not a coincidence." She sketched the outline of the burial mound.

"So, what, you think the killer chose the golf course because of the burial mound? Some kind of statement? Showing us he's familiar with the territory or something?" I pointed to the spot roughly where the dead man's head had popped up out of the ground. She marked it with an *X*.

"No, I'm saying, what if it's about the geography?"

"Meaning?"

"What else is unique to this spot?" Her eyes had gone flat. *Fear?*

I flicked a finger off the steering wheel for each possibility. "Let's see. Golf course, check. Bona fide burial mound, check. I'd say that's plenty unique for a murder site. What am I missing?"

"Oh, I don't know, the fact that your own lot just happens to sit awfully close to the same hole?" She pointed at the general location on the envelope.

My ears started ringing. "There's no way ..." *Is there?* "No one knows I own that lot. I mean unless they checked the tax records." I searched my memory. Images of attending my aunt's funeral popped up, followed by a hazy frame of me sitting in front of an attorney's desk. I remembered him telling me to transfer the deed into my name. But I didn't remember ever getting around to it. "Georgi, I just don't see how anyone could know it's mine. Seems like quite a stretch."

"You're not that hard to track, Chief." Georgi folded her arms across her chest.

"What do you mean?" My mind roved over the fire pit I'd had built on the empty lot. "Crap."

"Yeah. We're not the quietest bunch of rednecks when you invite us over to enjoy the stars and a campfire on your fancy golf course lot." Georgi hugged herself as if warding off a freezing gale.

"No, I guess not. And I don't want to start thinking about the long list of enemies I've created over the years." The hairs at the nape of my neck quivered as I turned down the drive toward my remote, rustic getaway in the woods.

Georgi had nothing to say to that.

CHAPTER SIX

When we stepped into the cottage and Georgi locked the door, her hands were shaking.

I plopped my purse on the kitchen island and started rummaging around on the counter behind me for coffee supplies. "The usual?"

"Please." She looked out the front windows, arms crossed. Fresh pine scent floated in through a window I'd left open last night. "Love it out here this time of year." She pointed up at an eagle's nest resting high above in the crooked pine boughs. "Still there."

"Yup. My lucky duck." I got the coffee brewing, then came over to glance up at the empty nest. I rested my hand on her shoulder. "We'll figure this out."

Georgi mustered a smile. "You've sure got it good out here, Josie." A bank of windows faced Devil's Lake on the far side of the great room. She walked toward them as if in a trance.

"Yup. Home sweet home." I picked up an eight-by-ten framed picture of Sam in her soccer uniform. "It'll be a lot more like home as soon as I bring her back here."

"Cliff bought her a fishing vest to match his. And a zombie-themed fishing pole." Georgi's eyes widened. "You'd tell me if she didn't really love it, right?"

I smiled. "Samantha loves fishing with Uncle Cliff. And I sure don't want to take her fishing, so let's leave well enough alone."

Georgi finally sat down on the sectional, letting go of a long breath.

"Tell me again why aren't you on the payroll, Georgi." I filled two mugs and joined her on the sofa.

"You can't afford me." She sipped her coffee.

"True that." I leaned forward to place my mug on the coffee table.

"Besides, that cop stuff is your specialty, not mine. Let's drop the murder for now, focus on my specialty for a while." A smug grin spread across her face.

"Yours being?" *Uh-oh. Did I just open the door I hadn't planned on opening today with her?*

"I thought you'd never ask. L-O-V-E. So, let's hear it. Now. All of it. Why have I not heard thing one from you relative to a certain gorgeous cop-type fellow?" She fluttered her lids at me like a fourteen-year-old.

I rolled my eyes. "Oh, for Pete's sake. It's complicated."

"No, it's really not. Mr. Practically Perfect is in love with you and has known you half your life, maybe more. You married an evil dude, who just got eviler over time. And then he died. Thank God and good riddance."

I looked away from her, eyes focused on the wall of windows and the greens and blues beyond. The vibrant colors blurred into each other. The trajectory of my marriage—its surprise ending and my husband's brutal death at the hands of a crazed serial killer—ran its course through my mind. Georgi had been loyal to the core throughout the entire ordeal, swooping in to nurse me back to health as my life fell apart before my eyes. She never tired of hearing me cry, listening to my fears, joining me in my grief.

She took my silence as permission. "Bad things happened, in so many ways. Our gorgeous Mr. Almost Perfect stepped in and stepped up. And instead of falling right into his open arms, like any other red-blooded American woman would've done, and probably every other woman in the world, you run in the opposite direction." She sliced a hand through the air, returning her attention to her coffee.

Heat rushed up my neck, burning over my cheeks. "Gah, ah ..." Glubs and gurgles instead of words came out. Not my finest moment. I cleared my throat and tried again. "You don't really know what went on between us. Uh, no ... uh, nobody really does." *All that effort, for that?*

Georgi narrowed her eyes. "Go on."

"Yeah, well, it's ... uh, complicated." Images of Nick's broad back, muscles rippling under his T-shirt while we worked out together, flowed through my mind like silk. An iron fist clamped around my heart.

"No, it's really not that complicated, Jo." Georgi's voice softened. "Isn't it time you stopped running?"

"I'm not running." I wrinkled my nose, closed my eyes. "Much." I was running. *I'm still running.*

She scooted over next to me and took my hand in both of hers. "Word of advice? Stop. Stand still long enough to take a good look at the man who's been right in front of you all along." Her words had tapered to a whisper.

My throat was a dry reed. I licked my lips and swallowed. "Where would I start after all that's happened since I pushed him away? And he hasn't exactly knocked himself out trying to get back in touch with me. Maybe he isn't interested in hearing from me anymore." My deepest fear unleashed.

"Yeah, maybe not. But you never know." Playfulness lifted her voice, danced through her eyes.

I cocked my head and rolled my hand forward. *Go on.*

"You should ask *him* about it." She folded her arms across her chest.

"Oh, really? And how and when would I do that?"

She looked at her wrist. "In about two hours. He's coming for dinner tonight."

"Nick? Here? Now?" My hand shook, sloshing coffee onto my jeans and the sofa. *Jeans. I'm wearing jeans. And they're tighter than they should be.* "I'm not ready for this. I need more time." I touched my chin, ran my hand over the slackening skin underneath it.

Georgi's laugh cascaded through the room. "Nick? No, not Nick, silly. Tom. And don't worry—you look great. He'll notice."

Tom! "Ah, that doesn't take much." Images assaulted me as I floundered to recover. Images of me wrapped up in hospital white, bandages hiding any skin the sheets revealed, Nick's chiseled features leaning over me, declaring his undying love for me. Memories of pushing him away with words, with gestures, stabbing at him with my red-hot fear. The beauty of his back as he walked away, leaving me alone with a morphine drip to quiet my regrets. "Whew. Glad it's Tom. I'm not sure I can handle the other one."

"Well, we've got a few hours to prep. What do you need? Booze? Prayer? A hand in the kitchen? He might be coming under the promise of one of your world-famous, home-cooked meals." Her hands seesawed in the air. "And by meal, I most certainly mean cake."

"What are we, back in junior high, setting each other up? You can't do this, Georgi. It's not right." But even as I whined at her, a pinprick of hope sparked in my heart. If just the thought of him stirred that much feeling, who knew? Maybe there was a chance for Nick and me. "Who called him? Or did he invite himself?"

"For what it's worth, he's been dropping us the occasional email, just to make sure you're alright—always asks about Sam—and wanting to know if you've mentioned him. He hasn't ever gone as far as to invite himself up or anything." She got her phone out of her purse and started thumbing through messages. "But when he sent this one, I decided to push the envelope." She handed me her phone.

Please tell her I said hello, and let her know I'm taking an interesting class with an old friend of hers at UW. And give Sammie my love.

"So, he's in Madison from time to time. A stone's throw from Baraboo and you think the geography gives you the right to meddle in peoples' lives?" I couldn't even drum up a false indignation. But thoughts of Nick eclipsed *everything*. Warmth was moving up my thighs, gaining in heat and force as it rose. *Sam. Does Nick still think about Sam?*

Tom. It'd be good to see him again. Maybe even great.

"Watching the sorrow in your eyes every time we talk about anything Nick-related gives me the right to meddle in your life. It's time to move on. You're being needlessly stubborn and uberly stupid. I thought maybe Tom could help." She got to her feet and stood in front of me on the sofa.

"That's not even a word." I held my hand out for her to help me up.

She smiled, took my hand, and pulled me to my feet. "What, *stupid*? Or *stubborn*? Yes, they are. I looked them both up and saw your picture on one and your name on the other." She hooked my elbow, steering me into the kitchen. "Besides, he's a nice guy, and you guys go way back. I can think of worse grounds for romance."

"Oh, for goodness' sake." I snorted, breaking both of us into giggles. "Fine. Let's get this party started." I put our mugs into the sink and turned around, leaning back against the counter. "But first, the big three." I cracked my knuckles. "One. What goes with pasta?"

"That's not one. That's actually three." Georgi squatted next to the island, reading cookbook spines on the shelves below.

"It is?" I opened my spice cabinet, starting an informal inventory, pulling out anything that smelled interesting and relatively fresh.

"Yep. You know better." She pulled out my favorite, written by a local chef with his own kitchen and Italian-themed dining room—a tiny hamlet only locals could find.

"Oh, dear." I looked down at myself. I was still wearing the clothes I had on during my impromptu golf outing that had morphed into an impromptu crime-scene investigation. Who knew what I'd brought into my own home? I groaned. "I'm hitting the shower. Open up to page two-fifty and start a shopping list. Bolognese." One of Nick's favorites. I sighed, shook my head. *Moving on.* I couldn't wait to fill my cabin with the delicious aroma—no matter who sat around my table.

"And for dessert? I had my heart set on this one." Georgi had the book opened wide, finger tapping the name of a dessert recipe.

I bent forward, reading the title. Marry Me Chocolate Flourless Cake.

I let the hot water roll over me while the wobbly dam that held my memories at bay broke open. Nick, pulling me into his arms. Nick, eyes sparkling with love over a candlelight dinner in my favorite Italian restaurant in downtown Chicago. Nick, crestfallen the day I told him I was marrying Del. Ruining everything.

For a season.

And now, not Nick, but Tom was back. *What do I wear for this?*

I rummaged through my perpetual-weekend wardrobe. Of all the times for Tom to drop back into my life, why'd he have to do it while I was on vacation in the north woods without access to a decent selection? I tried on the few options I'd packed, grimacing at the too-tight everything, settling on a pair of yoga pants with a skirt sewn onto them and a matching black top that showed off my toned arms. A cobalt cardigan topper would bring out my baby blues—while hiding the jiggles on the underside of said toned arms. *Michelle Obama, I'm not.* A pair of black flats completed the ensemble.

I looked at myself in the mirror. Flesh swung under my chin. Bags sagged under my eyes. Extra pounds rounded my belly under my careful disguise. My hair needed a touchup. What did he see in me? Would he be able to see it through all of *this*? Did his opinion even matter?

My dark thoughts lifted like steam, replaced by a glowing phrase. Biblical notions of God's faithfulness in the midst of man's overall disinterest came to mind. A prayer floated up from my heart, surrounding me with peace. *Thank you, Father. Forgive me for dissing the woman you made me to be. I know You're in control of all things, and I know You're bigger than my fear. Bigger than my thighs.* I smiled. *Lord, whatever this is, this thing between Nick and me, let it be of You. Your lead, God.*

I opened my eyes. The woman looking back smiled at me with shimmering eyes and a lovely face—weathered by pain but softened by grace. I smiled at her. *We got this!* I finished my makeup with artisan flair and strode into the kitchen.

Georgi was gone, presumably shopping. Pulling out my soup pot for the pasta reminded me of the many times Nick and I had poured out our life stories over a meal together during the dozen or so years we'd known each other. *How many times do people in our lives get under our skin and stay there?*

I busied myself setting the table for what was to come when Tom and Cliff finally walked through my door. I wished he were Nick instead of Tom. Maybe Georgi was right. Maybe now *was* time to stop running from Nick and start saying yes to the real deal.

CHAPTER SEVEN

I was carefully lifting the stencil off my shapely Marry Me Flourless Chocolate Cake when the doorbell chirped. Ignoring the sound of spring birds flitting through my home, I pulled the plastic stencil all the way off and admired my handiwork. Delicate flowers etched in confectioner's sugar graced the top of the culinary masterpiece. The perfect finish for our dinner.

I popped my head up and yelled. "C'mon in, Georgi. I'm up to my elbows in cake."

Another round of chirping hit me as I rinsed my hands in the sink. "Georgi?" A sliver of alarm ran through me, and I looked out the window. Her car wasn't in the driveway. I turned toward the front door.

A tall shadow wavered on the other side of the opaque glass window. Not Georgi tall. Tom and Cliff then? I opened the heavy wooden door. My stomach dropped to my feet, and my blood was an ice-cold sauvignon blanc.

"Nick." His name escaped my desert-sand throat. My eyes locked onto his, and I stood in the iron grip of his gaze. My heart constricted … and then opened like a hothouse rose. I took a deep breath and counted to three, managing only a whisper as I exhaled.

"Nick." His scent, mixed with the pines and damp earth of spring, was my elixir. Desire strengthened my limbs, loosened my muscles enough to shake my head and awkwardly offer him my hand. What would Emily Post suggest for greeting the man you loved and had walked away from—twice?

Nick decided for me. Closing the gap between us, he put his luxuriously muscled arms around me and pulled me against him, into his glorious strength. He sighed, opening up the tiniest space, drawing me closer still and rested his chin on my head.

I hoped he couldn't see my roots, but the way he quivered in my arms convinced me he wasn't thinking about that. I relaxed into him and wrapped myself around him, in awe of the perfect fit of his arms, his body against mine. *Welcome home.*

He loosened his grip, sliding an arm out from around me as we walked inside. After closing the door, he whirled me before him, cupped my chin in his hands and kissed me so tenderly, I wasn't sure he had. He'd been here less than a minute, and already I was dizzy and overwhelmed by the beauty and sheer majesty of him.

"I thought you might need a little help." His grin spread into his trademark smile.

"And this is how you're going to help?" I threw him a wobbly gesture with my right hand, leaving my left around his rock-hard waist.

He took my hand in his, interlocking our fingers. His brown eyes glowed with love, and heat I'd only hoped would still be there.

I raised our clenched hands and straightened mine out, pressing our palms together. His presence plunged me down twin paths of memories and hopes for a shared future. I damped my hopes down, marveling at the sight of his long, tawny fingers outlining mine.

We stood together in the heart of my cabin, palm-to-palm, gazing into each other's eyes. Hot chocolate laced with peppermint schnapps poured through my veins. Zaps of joy, lust, and sheer pleasure ran through me, interrupting the haze. My mind had forgotten the power of his body next to mine. Apparently, the rest of me had not.

He clasped his fingers around mine, brought my hand to his lips and gently kissed the back of my hand. I closed my eyes to break the spell. Skillful fingers lifted my chin, turning my face to meet his lips. *Lightning. French éclairs. Riding at full gallop under a moonlit sky in late September. Nick.*

"I missed you." He clasped his hands behind my back, soft brown eyes boring into mine. "I really, really missed you." He leaned in and kissed my forehead.

I pulled back, gliding my hands over his sinewy arms, remembering. "I ... I missed you too."

"So, what are we going to do about it?" He moved in to kiss me again.

Mechanical birds chirped. Nick tensed and stepped back.

I sucked in air, watching the doorknob turn.

Georgi's head peered around the knotty pine door. "Hey, kids, I'm home!" Her gleaming eyes landed on me first, and I knew then she'd made up the whole story about Tom. *Great. What will she and Cliff take over next?*

But confusion rolled across her face as Nick rushed over and pulled a bag of groceries from each arm. "Let me take those off your hands, Georgi."

I couldn't help admiring the muscle definition in his forearms and biceps as he placed the bags on the island. His movements reminded me of a panther. Sleek, muscular, and lethal.

Georgi wasn't seeing the beauty in his movement. She stared in blank-faced silence from her empty arms to Nick and slowly turned her head in my direction. I squinted back her, throwing my palms up, hoping to signal her to be cool 'til we could talk. Something was obviously not okay.

Nick didn't seem to mind. Calling out ingredients as he pulled them out of the grocery bags, he arranged them thoughtfully on the counter. I put the bags away and poured

Georgi another cup of coffee. She sat at the counter, watching us as we fell into a comfortable synchronicity in the kitchen.

I put a pot of water on to boil, pouring in a shot of olive oil and a pinch of salt. Nick set two boxes of pasta next to me on the counter. Hearing him pull my ancient cutting board out of the cabinet next to the stove prompted me to move the chocolate cake over to the coffee table. He'd need free rein and plenty of space to peel, chop and dice the vegetables to his liking.

Twenty minutes later, the beautiful aroma of sautéing garlic, leeks, and onions wafted throughout my little cabin. I washed and tore up a head of buttery Bibb lettuce and mixed it with a head of red leaf.

"You're not really combining those, are you?" Nick stood behind me, his velvety tones next to my ear.

My Midwestern sensibilities broke the spell, prompting me to carp at him. "You're not really going to tell me how to make a salad, are you?" I faced him, smiling. "Not unless you want to finish it for me."

He hated making salads. Something about the texture of the lettuce bugged him. "Allow me." He swooped in next to me, fussily separating the leaves. "The Bibb lettuce will do much better with a green goddess dressing. And the red leaf will be just right with oil, vinegar, a little lemon, and some sea salt. Why don't you join Georgi on the other side of the counter, and let me finish up in here?" He put his hands on my hips and steered me away from the kitchen.

"My mama didn't raise no fool. I'm good with that arrangement." I rummaged through the fridge and pulled out a bottle of chilled Ferrari. I popped the cork, poured three glasses, slid one over to Nick and took two to the sofa overlooking the lake. "C'mon, Georgi. Let's give the man his space."

Nick sang quietly in the background. I tasted the wine and smiled at Georgi. Her face was whiter than it should have been. The blank-faced stare had returned, and she didn't touch her wine.

Alarm rang through me. She didn't have her phone in sight. Had something happened to Cliff?

I leaned forward and whispered, "What's wrong, sweetie?"

She shot me an ashen glance, matching her low tone to mine. "I told you. Cliff's mystery dinner date for you tonight was supposed to be *Tom*. Not Nick."

"Quinn?" Was he really on his way here with Cliff? Images of both Quinn and Nick whirled together in an awkward dance, building to a crescendo in my living room. We all knew who would be standing after the last notes wound down. I looked at Georgi and shook my head. "You couldn't make this stuff up. So, who invited Nick?"

Georgi shrugged.

I rubbed my temples and exhaled. "So now what? Who calls Quinn off, you or me?"

"It might not be that easy." She clenched her teeth, flexing her jaw muscles. "Pretty sure they're on the road already."

"I don't care. Call him off." I forgot to whisper the last part. Silence rocketed through the air. Nick stopped singing. *Crap*.

"No, don't," Nick said. He stood behind the counter, wearing one of my aprons and holding a wooden spoon. "Quinn and I can get along. As long as he doesn't try to steal the affections of the woman I love and doesn't try to tell me how to run my investigation."

His words blasted through me. *The woman I love.* Was I still *his* after nearly two months of no contact and less than fifteen minutes of a surprise reunion?

"Investigation? What investigation?"

"Yeah, what do you know that we don't know?" Georgi sang out to Nick with the voice of a woman and the heart of a teenager.

"Wait," I said. "I don't want to do this."

"Sure, you do," Georgi urged. "You might want to knock back a little more of that vino though. Could get interesting around here." She looked at her phone. "In about five minutes. Give or take."

"So that's it? We host our own private showing of *Boa vs. Python* right here in my living room?" I rose to my feet, air squeezing out of constricted lungs.

"Yeah. Pretty much. What's not to love about that?" Georgi's fingers were twitching on the stem of her wineglass, turning it back and forth.

"Good grief. I've had fun before, Georgi, and this ain't gonna be fun."

"Maybe not for *you.*" She chortled.

"Nick? Are we okay?" I looked up at him, still gorgeous in my apron, deftly turning a counter full of vegetables and meat into something savory. *Twenty minutes into the game, and I'm hoping for what—a promise of good behavior? What's wrong with me?*

He broke into a brilliant smile, eyes sparkling. "You and I are much more than okay—and the rest of the evening will be pleasant. Maybe better than pleasant."

Sensory overload. Warmth spread through me. The sound of his voice coupled with those stunning brown eyes had sent me over the edge before. But that was long ago. Wasn't it? I stared at him, dumbstruck.

His smile broadened. "And don't we have some business to discuss over dinner? I want to hear Quinn's take on your golfer. I respect his opinion on this and the other scenes. Crime techs should have a preliminary report sent to him before he gets here. Makes this a working dinner." He stepped around the counter and leaned against it, facing us.

He had my attention now. And it wasn't just the way he filled out my apron. If the Bureau were interested in the DB I'd found today, there was something else going on. "So, you wanna fill us in on the Bureau's role? And what you mean by *scenes*? Or do we have to wait for a rousing game of Pictionary after dinner?"

"You haven't grown in patience in the last few months." He looked at his watch.

"Nor you in clarity." I cocked an eyebrow at him.

Gravel shifted under tires outside, announcing the arrival of Cliff and Quinn.

The car came to a stop, and both front doors popped open. *This oughta be fun.*

CHAPTER EIGHT

Cliff and Quinn walked up the hill from the carport, gesturing and alternating between smiles and scowls. Probably talking shop. Not of the cop-shop variety either. They shared a deep affinity for the virtues of cherry for handcrafting furniture over the evils of pine, the poor man's alternative. Their love for all things outdoors that could be dragged indoors to become, or be placed upon, a table, had been cemented in their high school Woods and Metals class.

Which was where we all had met—really! I stuck with the class for almost three whole days. Long enough to gather intel on the hot guys and to determine life would lead us in different directions. Georgi had already fallen in love with elements of design by then, and Cliff had fallen in love with her. Quinn and I went along for the ride, and we were all still friends, fifteen-some years later. *Pushing twenty years.*

I smiled at the thought of what I'd come to think of as our black swan moment. The day we met seemed predictable enough—four like-minded country kids making fun of our teacher and trying to be cool while we checked out our classmates. We didn't hear the levers of our lives clicking into place, or feel the lathe shaping our futures by gathering the four of us atop sawdust-covered floors. History in the making—who knew?

Georgi opened the door and waited for them, leaving Nick and me standing alone at the kitchen island. He placed his hand on my forearm. "You're more beautiful than ever, Jo. It feels like home being next to you again. I'm sorry for the silence."

I pulled up mental pictures of my too-tight jeans, then pushed them all aside. "Thanks. I … I don't know what to say. It feels like a dream." *Dream or nightmare? What will happen with him and Quinn around the same table?* Nick's big-city upbringing hadn't instilled much respect for a small town sheriff who preferred well-broke cowboy boots over fine Italian-leather loafers. Quinn's penchant for hiding his intellect behind his run-down pickup truck and on-again-off-again country dialect had caused Nick to underestimate him more than once over the years. Years ago, the three of us had worked a case together that slipped across the state line. While we'd solved the case, we never did resolve our complicated relationship triangle.

Flames swept across my cheeks as I recalled another long ago incident. This one had involved a gang of Colombian drug dealers rumored to have made it to the Flambeau Flowage area of Northern Wisconsin. Having combed the woods for hours with a bevy of agents, canines, and helicopters, Nick called off the search. An hour later, Quinn collared the thugs hiding out in the back end of a bear cave.

I could think of several ways this evening might end, and none of them was too "pleasant."

Quinn and Georgi hugged at the door, Quinn's gaze reaching in to see me and noticing Nick. He squinted and turned his eyes away. *Nightmare it will be.*

"Quinn," I said, "I … I didn't know you were coming. But it's a lovely surprise." I placed myself in front of him, forcing the hug.

"Looks like today is full of surprises." He nodded toward Nick, offering his hand. "Nick."

Nick clasped his hand. "Good to see you, man. Sounds like we've got a lot of catching up to do on our case."

Our case?

"Don't it? Never thought I'd say it, but I'm glad to catch the two of you in the same room at the same time." Quinn smiled, eyes grim.

Huh? Had I imagined him flirting with me a few short hours ago?

I went to the fridge, pulled out a bottle of Spotted Cow and handed it to Quinn. "Here you go. Now come on in and cut the mystery. I'm getting a distinct feeling you boys may know more than I do about my little discovery on the sixth hole."

Nick grabbed a platter of veggies, hummus, and assorted chips and headed toward the sectional facing the lake. We joined him, Quinn sitting in one corner, Nick in the other. Cliff, Georgi, and I sat next to each other in the middle. Closest to the platter.

I grabbed a fistful of Nacho Cheese Doritos. *You can take the girl out of the country ...*

"Alright." I decided to take command. "Let's all agree to ignore the fact this impromptu reunion is at once beautiful and crazy awkward, and let's decide to make the most of it."

"Who's cooking?" Quinn looked from Nick to me.

"I'm on the pasta," Nick said, "and Jo's on the dessert. Right, sweetie?" He looked over at me and winked. *Really, Nick? In front of everyone?*

Cliff's face brightened.

"And tell us about the dessert, Josie." Georgi jumped in quick.

"Ah, it's uh, a flourless chocolate cake." A Marry Me Flourless Chocolate Cake.

"Good enough for me. Keeping my weapon holstered. At least 'til dessert's over." Quinn said. "Now that we've got basic safety procedures out of the way, why don't you fill us in on why you're here, Nick?"

"There's another reason why you're here?" I frowned and glanced at Nick. He looked back at me through hooded lids, and his lips grew taut.

I turned my gaze back to Quinn, willing him to fill me in. "Go on."

"Not my story to tell." Quinn took a long draw from his bottle and looked away.

"Oh, for Pete's sake, out with it." I glared at Nick.

Nick and Quinn exchanged quick glances. Crimson flashed across Quinn's cheeks and disappeared. Nick took a drink from his bottle.

"Georgi, Cliff, do you guys know all about it too?" I nudged them with my elbows from my convenient perch between them.

"Not yet." Georgi sat back on the sectional, crossing her legs.

"Nope. But I got a feeling I'm about to." Cliff scooped hummus onto a plate and settled back into the folds of the sofa.

"Alright, guys." I turned to Nick. "We'll start with you. You came here for a reason. Knowing you, the timing is anything but accidental, and you had to know I had company. So, I'm guessing you don't mind sharing your story in front of said company. Especially since you and Quinn here seem to have become something of an item." I couldn't hide the irritation in my voice.

My goading unleashed Nick. *Finally.* He pulled his velvety brown eyes away from the lake.

Lava rolled slowly through my stomach. Gears clicked into place in my mind. This must be what Quinn had been shushing Bhatt about earlier today. How long had they been working together on this new case?

"A string of murders occurring in Wisconsin, involving only victims from Illinois, caught our collective eye. Some of my buddies at the Bureau are of the opinion there could be some sort of redneck rivalry element at work here."

"Hmph." Georgi shot me a look that all but screamed *I told you so.*

"*Redneck*'s a little harsh." Quinn's defensive tone surprised me. "And way too premature to call. What I would say is that there seems to be an interstate element to the crimes."

"If this little killing spree predates my golfer, what's the timeline, and what's the body count?" A white spark of curiosity emerged, followed by a flash of shame. Quinn had been ready to tell me more at the crime scene, and I'd distracted him. Made it all about *me. Rats. Will I ever grow up?*

"Three." Quinn put up three fingers.

Nick shook his head. "Four, counting the golfer."

Quinn nodded. "Last week, some guy plugged a man from Rockford, Illinois, while he was stopped on Highway 33 between Portage and Baraboo. Week before that, another guy, this time from Buffalo Grove, Illinois, was beaten to death and left in a soybean field outside of Westfield. Highway 51."

"And in the first one, we think, a man from Oak Park, Illinois, was drowned during a midnight ice-fishing expedition up near Crandon. Each one of the murders was well-planned and staged to look like something other than what it was. And each one was linked. By letters." Nick thumbed through his cell phone. "We almost missed the first calling card. Subtle." He got up and held his phone out to me.

"Wisconsin state boys did miss it at the first scene. It was Slick here who put it together." Quinn smirked at his nemesis, waiting for me to study the picture. "And that wasn't until the second scene was being processed."

An ice-covered lake at night, brightly lit, threw whites and blacks and shadows everywhere. There was a perfectly round hole in the ice with a wide circle of yellow tape surrounding it, lettered crime-scene markers carefully placed on the ice.

"It seems pretty routine." The body had been removed. Cops milled about in the photo.

"How many evidence markers do you see?" Nick asked.

"I don't know. They're lettered, hang on. Five? Six?" I wasn't seeing a connection.

"What color are they?" Nick sank back into his corner of the sectional.

"Yellow and black. Except for one, and it's white and black. That important?" A tingling ran through me. "And it's not in the right order. There are six letters, *A* to *F*, but this is a different color, and it's the letter *J*."

"Check out the next couple of pics."

I thumbed to a picture of a field. Remnants of snow and ice clung to brown leaves. No body, no cops. I thumbed on and saw a close-up picture of a square, white bead with the letter *E* printed in black on it. "This looks pretty close to the bead we found on my golfer today."

"Don't it, though?" Quinn came alive. "And look at the next shot."

A wave of dizziness flowed over me. What kind of bizarre clues were these? The next frame contained another close-up. This one featured the word *ME*, printed in ragged black letters on a white background.

"What the heck?" I looked up at Quinn, then over to Nick. "This looks like something torn off a magazine cover or something. So, what do you make of it?"

"Think about it. If you piece it together, it could be a message. A deadly message." Quinn's words floated in the air. I visualized the numbers and the letters next to each other.

"*J-E-ME* ... What's that supposed to mean?" Neither man offered any ideas. "Either we're missing a few letters, or this isn't anything."

"There any more to this story?" I looked at Quinn, then to Nick. What were they leaving out? Besides the fact that they'd been in touch behind my back.

Nick turned toward me, loosely crossing his legs at the ankle. "We think the killer knows his geography. We traced the bullet trajectory from the highway shooting up to a bluff where the shooter had been waiting, belly to the ground, watching the cars go by. Based on the food wrappers and spent ammo, he probably spent a few afternoons up there, sighting his scope, testing out his rifle. Dress rehearsals." Nick looked over at Quinn.

"At first, I thought he was nuts. But now I think his theory's got legs." Quinn nodded at Nick. *Continue.*

"Killer had to have twenty-twenty vision, nerves of steel, and the patience of Job. Even with all that, it'd be nearly impossible to take out a guy with Illinois plates, going down the road at sixty-some miles per hour in broad daylight. Until one unlucky man from Buffalo Grove, Illinois, just happens to have some kind of car trouble along the same stretch of road. Thus, becoming victim number three." Nick said. "And how many guys would know where to find the perfect kill spot up on Pigtail Alley?"

"Pigtail Alley?" I remembered the feel of raw, equine power flowing underneath me, Red Chief and me scaling the ridge for the sheer joy of it. Fifteen years ago? Twenty? "Local boy?"

"Who else would know about the deer trails winding up and down the ridge? Whoever it was didn't leave much of a trail." Quinn tapped his fingers against his thigh.

I voiced my thoughts. "How could he have known the guy would stop on the highway? Did he know the victim? Was this a random hit, or did the shooter somehow set him up? Maybe had a partner working the road for him?"

"I think so," Nick said. "Had to have been working with someone non-threatening enough to cause the vic to pull over."

Amateur … or trying to look like one by leaving lots to go on at the crime scene." Nick got up, reached the stove in three strides, stirred the red sauce, and adjusted the heat. "And what kind of hunter uses a semiautomatic rifle to kill Bambi?"

"Plenty of 'em." Cliff joined in. "You don't want to know."

I nodded. "Sad but true. So, the guy used a semiautomatic. Any luck with the DNA tests?" I pictured the top of the ridge. I'd been up there many times.

"No," Quinn said. "Everything came back clean. He camped out at the clearing. There were two shots fired. That we can verify from casings found at the scene."

"Nobody gets that lucky from that distance," Nick said. "He knew what he was doing, who he wanted to shoot. And if he was up there more than once, who knows how many actual rounds he may have gone through. If he were a careful man, he'd have picked up after himself on the other trips too." He pulled plates out of cupboards, placing a stack of five on the island.

"Military?" I asked. "Shooter like that has to have a history." I pictured the distance from the side of the road to the killer's perch. "Quinn's geography theory has to be right. Killer either knew the car, or he was waiting for the right license plate to come along. It's out there, but we might as well put it on the table until we can eliminate it. Or come up with something better."

Georgi leaned forward, looking from me to Quinn. "So, some guy was hanging out on the top of Pigtail Alley with a high-powered rifle, watching the highway for a car with Illinois plates, ready to shoot whoever was driving it?"

"That's a pretty accurate summary." Nick chimed in from the kitchen.

"Four bodies in four weeks?" The Mac truck weight of it all hit me, hard.

"Yeah, pretty much." Quinn's jaw ticked. His tell.

No wonder he'd called Nick in. He was in way over his head.

So much for my doctor-ordered vacation. And my reunion with Nick.

What was it they said about a woman scorned?

CHAPTER NINE

"Four bodies in four weeks, you two team up out of the blue, and not even a courtesy call my way?" Fog rolled around in my head. "What if I hadn't gone golfing this morning? Would I still be in the dark?" It was a cheap shot, childish even, but I was ticked. And they were in my house, around my table.

Sparks nipped my spine. I stood and went to Nick in the kitchen, hands on hips. "What made *you* decide to just show up here today? Did Quinn call you?" Heat flushed my cheeks. Could I really accuse them of working together behind my back? Did they have any obligation to tell me what they were doing?

"I thought inviting him here might be the fastest way to catch us all up to speed at once." Quinn surprised me for the second time today.

"*You* invited him?" I pointed at him, my face wrinkling into an angry scowl. I willed my face to loosen. I had to relax my brows, or those worry lines I'd been noticing lately might decide to stay.

"And you know I've always enjoyed a good mystery." Nick put a lid on the saucepot and turned down the burner.

They didn't really owe me anything. I knew that. I was just … what? Jealous? Desirous? Spoiled—wanting to be the center of attention? Or a good cop wanting to get to the bottom of the dead guy messing up my bogey on the sixth hole?

"And mysteries never cease around you, do they?"

Georgi topped off her wine glass, handed her husband a bottle of Spotted Cow, and headed for the door. "Honey, let's enjoy a moment together out on the porch."

"Right behind ya."

"And then there were three." Quinn watched them leave and came into the kitchen.

"When did you boys get so cozy together?" I pulled out a stool and sat down at the island. "And why?" I glared at Nick.

"Contrary to popular belief, my world didn't stop turning when a certain beautiful chief of police asked me to stop pursuing her. I was going to drown my sorrows in expensive liquor and start playing piano bars in Paris, maybe ask for a transfer, take up a teaching gig at Quantico for a month or so. But then Chase Lafferty up and died of a heart attack."

"The FBI profiler?"

"The same. I was invited to take his place teaching a few special seminars in Mad Town." He pulled a stool around the island and sat down to face me.

"And, hick investigator that I am and lifelong fan of the deceased, I had a front row seat in his class." Quinn pointed his bottleneck at Nick.

I pursed my lips, brows arched high.

"I wasn't exactly thrilled to see your secret-agent man teaching the class I'd waited weeks to take." Quinn flicked his eyes at me and then looked down at his beer bottle.

"Teaching this class was the best way to keep myself sane and in the game. After leaving you alone in the hospital that night ..." The tremor in Nick's voice stirred a torrent of self-blame within me. Silence enshrouded us. Were we all remembering how close I'd come to being murdered by a crazed killer? I had a feeling Nick hadn't yet forgiven himself for leaving me alone in the hospital room that day. Was that what had kept him from finding me sooner? Guilt or shame?

Either way, powerful forces like that could destroy a man from the inside out.

"In any case, the minute our killer chose to mess with the Bureau of Indian Affairs, he chose to work with me."

"Oh, yeah. I forgot all things Native American are federal affairs. Lucky you. Wait a minute. Could triggering the Bureau's involvement be intentional?"

The men looked at each other. "Seems like a strong possibility," said Quinn.

An uneasy détente settled around us. I'd grown up with Quinn—he was the brother I'd never had. Nick and I shared a complicated past I hoped one day might form a solid future. But it was a future I didn't believe I deserved. So, I'd married someone I thought I did deserve. And now with all the detritus of my near-death experience, and me being such a selfish baby, half the—*baby!*

Samantha! A glance at my watch told me Samantha would be going to bed soon.

"I gotta make a call. You two talk among yourselves." I jumped off the stool and hurried down the hall behind the kitchen into my bedroom, closing the door behind me. In the excitement of the day, while I thought about Sam constantly, I hadn't found a minute to call her.

She answered on the first ring. "Hey! Where you been?" Her voice carried sorrow and the question of her life. *You're coming back for me, right?*

I winced, shut my eyes tight and offered a quick prayer. *Please God, give me wisdom. Let me show Samantha my forever love ... and Yours.* "Baby, you're always with me—in my heart and on my mind—no matter how far apart we are. I love you, Sam. Wild horses couldn't keep me away from you."

"Zombies neither?" Her voice relaxed, transforming her from a wizened old woman back into her seven-year-old self.

"Zombies neither. Not even giant wild boars." We'd spent a day hunting priceless objets d'art through the central Wisconsin countryside last fall. Our highlight had been a pair of house-sized wild boars, jumping over an impossibly large fence, meticulously sculpted out of innumerable bales of straw. The pair graced brochures for the event, becoming an overnight sensation on last year's Farm Art D'Tour. *Only in Wisconsin.*

She giggled. "When are you coming back?"

"Soon, sweetie. And then you're coming here to spend time with Uncle Cliff and Aunt Georgi and me." I moved the conversation forward, asked about her foster family's new puppy, shielding my heart—and Sam's—from thoughts of Nick. I knew how sad it'd make her if she knew he was here and he hadn't even asked about her.

More giggling. A dropped phone. "Sophie, no!" A happy girl sighing.

"Sounds like somebody's getting kiss-attacked." I pictured the taupey-gold fur ball.

"Sophie says come home soon. She misses you."

"I love you, Sam. Let me talk to your foster mom now, okay?"

"I love you, Mama. And so does Sophie. Come back." She slipped the last words out and retreated from me. *Footsteps running.*

After checking in with the crazy-generous couple with Texas-sized hearts who'd fostered Sam for months, I ended the call and sighed. *Hold on baby, just a little while longer. Mama's coming.* I sat on my bed, watching the waves shimmer off Devil's Lake. The pull of the waves drew me back to another place and time.

I closed my eyes and gave in to the luxury of sweet dreams for several seconds. My thoughts reached back to a golden afternoon Nick, Sam, and I had spent together, cooking and coloring and laughing in front of a fire. I'd have staked my shield on Nick's commitment to making our happy little family permanent. We had fit. We were all in love, tenderly making our way to each other. It was perfect. Too bad it was only in my head.

Too bad I'd pushed perfect away before my release from the hospital. Too bad perfect hadn't come back, hadn't waited around to help me through recovery, to hold Sam while she cried herself to sleep at night. Too bad perfect was just another pale horse passing through our lives.

Was it too late for us? After everything we'd lost, was there any chance at all of redeeming this love? Could Nick and I wrap our hearts around each other and reclaim lost time? Warmth rushed over me, and I closed my eyes. A beautiful vision of Nick and me pulling Samantha solidly into our hearts and creating a forever family blossomed in my mind. In my vision, I was beautiful and sure, smiling at the future, finally able to invite the fantasy family out of my head and into my life—to stay.

With God, all things are possible. I turned the tried-and-true verse from Matthew around in my mind like a prism, thoughts igniting off the angles in my mind. As I blinked open my eyes, the thoughts evaporated, leaving me with a feeling of peace and the assurance of being deeply loved.

CHAPTER TEN

I sucked in air and blew out, rounding the corner into the heat of the kitchen. Way too much heat. Too much to handle? *We'll see.* The men looked up. Cliff had joined them.

"How is she?" Nick stared at me.

Is it any of your business anymore? His hi-def gaze brought goosebumps up and down my legs. I didn't owe him anything, right? Sam wasn't *ours*. Just mine. And I was a fierce protector of my own. Nick should have remembered that.

"She's fine."

Cliff surprised me by jumping in. "You wouldn't recognize her. She's growin' right up. Gonna be my fishing buddy."

Nick turned away, struck by an urgent need to stir a different pot.

"And a Packers fan." Cliff pulled out his phone, thumbed through pictures, pulled up a series featuring him, Georgi, Sam, and me at Lambeau Field.

I snorted, shaking my head. "That was a blast and a half. Sammie still wears her jersey to bed too."

"She loved that jersey, didn't she?" Cliff beamed.

I nodded, smiling. "She loves it. And we're still enjoying reminiscing about the spanking the Pack gave the Bears. Almost as good as the brats." Sharing recollections of our family moments in front of Nick and Quinn felt awkward.

"How you doing on beer, Cliff? Ready for another?" I grabbed his half-full bottle, tossed it in the recycle bin, and walked to the fridge without waiting for a response.

Nick clanked a lid on the sauce pot. "I really would like to see any new pictures of Sam you've got. I miss her. How's she doing, really?"

He turned around, faced me and trained his impossibly beautiful eyes on me, pulling me into his orbit. I snapped my eyes shut, trying to break the spell Nick cast over me just by being near. I opened them with a slight shake of my head, willing away his magic.

I stared at Nick's perfectly formed lips, hunger roiling through me. *Out of the frying pan* ... Life flickered through me in places I'd thought long dead. Warm apple-pie images flicked through my mind, followed by peonies opening in the early days of June. Only it wasn't that precious floral scent wafting through me. It was Giorgio. It was Nick.

Cliff leaned over to take the beer still dangling from my fingertips, popped the cap and walked out saying something about finding out where Georgi had disappeared to.

Nick moved like silk around the counter, inserting himself between Quinn and me, lethal good looks draining away my resolve. He stood so close, I felt the rhythm of his breathing, and I wanted for all the world to feel his arms around my waist, his lips on my skin. Heat flowed over my face, my heart jackhammering through my ribs, through my temples.

Nick brushed his forearm against mine, sending liquid fire through me. Ringing in my ears distracted me as Quinn mumbled something about having to get back to the office. He kept his eyes lowered as he stepped back from the counter, grabbed his jacket off a stool and walked out the door in a haze of white noise. The tongue of the door's lock clicked into place, cracking like a rifle in the winter. Strong arms circled my waist from behind, and the tall, slender, delicious warmth of Nick enveloped me. I leaned back into him, wrapping his arms tighter around me, closed my eyes, and sighed.

So much for being mad at him.

We stood as one. Me, leaning deeper into him. Nick, resting his chin on the top of my head, drawing me ever tighter. His heart beat against my spine, pulsing throughout every fiber of my being, sending shimmering waves of heat through me.

"Josie, my Josephine. I've missed you so, so much." He kissed my head, holding me.

"Are you really here?" I let myself fall deeper into him. "With me?" *Are you here to stay?*

"I've always been here with you. Sometimes more visibly than others." He breathed into my hair.

I felt his ribs expand and contract with the rhythm of his breathing. Peace, sureness, a solid sense of *yes* emanated throughout my body, mind, and soul.

And *want. I want this. I want this man. I want us. I want. And wanting is a good thing.*

I pulled his right hand up to my lips and kissed it, then leaned my head back and crooked my neck into his chin. Sighing out his name, I closed my eyes.

"Let's clear things up between us?" Nick said, sliding his hands from my shoulders to my waist. One palm touched my bare skin, I stopped breathing.

Nick turned me to face him, placing a finger under my chin, gently tilting my head up. He waited for my eyes to find his before continuing. "Josephine Oliver, I've given you everything you said you wanted—time and space apart. I promised you this, and I've given it to you. You asked me to give you some breathing room, time to think things through, and I did. But seasons change. And that time—our season of separation—it's time for that season to come to an end." Masculine eyes bored into mine as he edged closer, thighs touching mine, and curled his right leg around my left, pulling me into him. "My Josephine."

I gasped, turning my face to meet his. Love and desire radiated from him like a tropical rainstorm. I stretched onto my tiptoes, needing to feel his lips again.

I. Want. This. Man.

I licked my lips, brushing them, feather-light, against his. He responded, teasing my lips with his, dancing his tongue over them before pressing his lips to mine. I kneaded my way through his muscular back, pleasure firing through my hands, warming other long-cold parts of my being.

My mind filled with sights and smells of velvety dark chocolate poured over sea-salt dotted caramels ... filet mignon, drizzled in a fine, dark glacé ... cinnamon, nutmeg apple pie wrapped in a hazelnut crust ... all leading me to delicious images of Nick's amazing body entwined with mine.

We took a reluctant breath.

"I don't want to make a bigger deal out of it than necessary, but Quinn and I are teaming up on this borderline killer."

My head snapped back, and I winced. "Whoa, so you're taking this Illinois-Wisconsin thing seriously?"

"Yes. So, should you." His jaw muscles twitched under his smooth skin.

"What's that supposed to mean?" Annoyance slipped under mine.

"It means you're the only one of us who has a foot in both worlds." I tried to pull away, but he held onto me. "Probably doesn't mean anything. But what if it does? I'm done taking chances with you, Josie."

Heat rolled off his body, snuggling around mine like a blanket. I sighed, feeling a dam of reserve break within me. He reached his arms around my hips and pulled me toward him.

Tiny stars burst across a dark sky in my mind. "I'm going to need a little time to get used to ..."

"No. No more time." His hands reached up my back, and my neck curled up in pleasure. He put his lips to my ears. "I'm back, baby." He gave a little nip, whispering, "Get used to it."

He ran his tongue slowly up the side of my ear, hot breath driving me wild. He kissed my earlobe and continued with soft kisses down the side of my face, reaching my lips.

And lingered.

"Ahem!" Georgi slammed a set of keys down on the counter like a hiker announcing her presence to the local grizzlies. "Okay, kids, that's enough!"

Nick and I broke apart, two high school kids caught necking in a basement. He smirked. I blushed.

Cliff closed the cabin door and made his way to the stove. "If you two are going to eat each other, Georgi and I will help ourselves to the pasta."

Nick and I shot apart like polarized magnets. White noise roared through my head, black-rimmed stars appearing and disappearing as I stared into his glorious eyes. Pulling my attention away from him to follow the sound, I beamed at the four place-settings Georgi had put out in the dining room.

She motioned us to our seats, and once we were all seated around the table asked Nick to do the honors.

"I'd be glad to. Let's pray." At Nick's words, we bowed our heads.

After his prayer, we enjoyed a fine meal and lively conversation, soul mates filling in the blanks, adding color and texture to the gaps in each other's histories. We kept to pastels and soft touches, as if by prearrangement, and I was glad. No need to get into the sharp angles and dead ends each of us harbored tonight. Plenty of time for those conversations when the need arose. And I planned to make good and sure the need would not arise tonight. Especially not between Nick and me. The sepia quality of candlelight added to the dreamlike feel of the moment. This was the kiss, the moment, and the man that I'd remember forever.

"Well, that was yummy!" Georgi giggled after the men left and we finished washing the dishes. Her willingness to make herself at home and spend the night delighted me.

I snapped a dish towel at her before hanging it up. She closed the dishwasher.

"Do you have any more of the sweet white wine?"

"I believe I do. Hold on." I rummaged around in the fridge, returned with the bottle of Ferrari, and topped off her glass.

"Okay, girl, you got some 'splainin' to do." She jabbed her head at the sectional sofa. "Let's go, sister."

We settled into the oversized splendor of the old sofa, staring at our reflections in the full-length windows. The flickers from the candles danced over the dark waters.

Georgi sipped her wine, eyes trained on mine. "So. what are you so afraid of, girl? You can't get better than this man."

Might as well jump right into it. "Yeah, well, I'm doing my best."

"See that you do this time. I don't want to go through another round of Josie-knows-best with this guy. He's a good man, who is clearly crazy about you. What could you possibly be afraid of?"

I took a deep breath and let it out. *Does she really want to know?* "Let's face it, Georgi—two weddings and a funeral don't exactly make me the prize hog at the county fair." My country roots were showing, but I didn't care.

"Forgettin' something, ain't ya?" Georgi jumped right into the pit with me.

I looked over at her, feeling my brows etch deep angles into my forehead.

"Two weddings and a funeral. Is that what you'd call it?" Amusement danced in her eyes.

"Ha! Almost. One wedding and two funerals, to be exact. All the more reason this thing with Nick is never gonna happen." I looked down to where my wedding ring used to live and shook my head. "How will I ever shake these doubts, Georgi?"

"That's more like it. Truth will out. Isn't that what you always say? Whatever that means."

"I know I oughta be a better woman, but I'm not. I know it wasn't his fault—I'm the idjit that pushed him away, but it's not like he fought that hard to stay, is it?" I shivered. "I know he's an amazing man, and yes, you may have a point—there might be a little chemistry alive and popping up every now and then—"

"A little? I can barely breathe when I'm around you two! A man is a terrible thing to waste, Josie—especially one as honorable as *yours*." She emphasized the word *yours* with a finger pointed in my direction.

"He's not mine. He, he's uh"—I fished for the right way to say it— "He's Nick Vitarello. He's his own man. He's not *my* man. I don't have a man. And I wasn't all that successful with the last one. So maybe it's time to quit while I'm behind." I tapped the rim of the can of diet ginger ale rolling between my hands.

"I don't buy it. And you're not giving him the credit he deserves—or yourself, for that matter. He's an amazing guy, and you're the catch of the century. Any man would be honored to have you. Even if you are a flight risk."

"You did *not* just go there." I rolled my eyes, leaned back in my chair and groaned.

"I did just go there. Why? You've got a man who's crazy about you, willing to face your hillbilly roots, who gets your world, and who's loved you since before you were born. At least since before you were married. And he came back for you. Twice. That has to mean something to you. And he didn't leave you. That's your past talkin'." There was an edge in her voice. Her eyes would be tear-filled any second now.

"He doesn't know what he doesn't know." I pressed the heels of my hands into my eyeballs, rubbing them over my head. "And I don't know how to tell him. I don't want to saddle him with my fear." Another look down at the ring that wasn't there convinced me I wasn't quite as far along on my healing path as I'd thought. I looked over at my best friend, eyes brimming with tears. "Turns out I might have a little more work to do on me."

CHAPTER ELEVEN

I woke up to the smell of bacon frying and a rich baritone voice singing an Italian aria. Nick. In my cabin. *Really?* Then a female voice, sparkling, happy. Georgi.

I pulled myself out of bed, threw on my Green Bay Packers' bathrobe and headed to the kitchen. Nick and Georgi stood shoulder to shoulder, laughing and reigning over two cast-iron skillets. The otherworldly aromas emanating from their direction told me theirs was another successful meeting of the culinary minds.

I cleared my throat. "You two want to be alone?"

"Not anymore." Nick threw a proprietary arm around Georgi's shoulders, took the spatula from her hand and turned to face me. "Morning, beautiful."

His silky-smooth voice rolled over me, sending warm tingles to all the right places. *After all these years, and two months of radio silence, he still has this effect on me?* "Um …" I was stammering. *Great.*

Georgi smiled, gently broke away from Nick, engulfed me in a hug and whispered in my ear. "Smooooth, sista."

I giggled. *Giggled? Get a grip.* Pulling away from Georgi, I linked my arm in hers and was immediately captured by Nick's eyes. "Yeah, well, good morning. And, uh, thanks for whatever it is you've got cooking up over there. Smells delicious."

"We've got a big day ahead of us. Gotta start it right with a tasty and nutritious breakfast." Nick fixed his gorgeous brown eyes on mine and winked.

Capillaries burst inside my cheeks. My heart pounded against my chest, and tiny beads of sweat broke out under my hairline. "I, uh, yeah." *Brilliant.*

"It's like you always say, beautiful—that killer's not going to catch himself." Nick tossed the spatula into the air, whirled around to face the stove and caught it behind his back. "Bam! I still got it, baby."

I shook my head, grateful for the reprieve, although I knew from experience that staring at his backside could prove equally distracting. "So, uh, learn anything new?" Was that why he came over here this morning? Had he heard something already? Maybe it wasn't my girlish figure and charm-school ways after all.

"Isn't there always something new to learn when I'm around you?" He raised one shoulder, and even that looked sexy to me.

Get a grip, Oliver. "Yeah, uh, I guess." I had to get my head out of the glory of Nick and back into the game. "So, what is it?" *Again, with the brilliant lines. What does he see in me, anyway?*

"Let's just say it's apropos of you to be wearing your Packers robe this morning." Georgi crossed her arms and leaned into me. She felt solid and real. I'd forgotten she was here.

I grimaced. "Go on."

Nick turned around and placed the skillet on a trivet in the center of the island.

"We'll get to that. But first, let's eat." He pulled up a stool, waiting for us to settle ourselves across the island from him. After offering thanks for our meal, he looked up—spatula in hand. "Bon appétit, ladies." He served Georgi and me generous portions before serving himself.

The waistband of my newest pair of straight-leg jeans danced through my mind. I placed my butter knife in the center of the egg mixture on my plate, visualizing what a fist of protein looked like. It looked like less than half of what was on my plate. I shook my head and looked up at an amused Nick. "So, you were saying?"

"I started playing with Georgi's Wisconsin-Illinois enmity idea." He took a bite. He was the only man I knew who looked even sexier eating. Especially at my kitchen counter.

Georgi nudged me in the ribs. "What, are you going to send half of your breakfast to starving children overseas or something?"

I closed my eyes and huffed. "Come to think of it, there are quite a few onions in this mix, right? And a piece or two of green pepper?"

"Oh, yeah. It's a veritable cornucopia of vegetables."

"You both get hotter every time I see you." Nick cut out a neat piece of hash browns, added a layer of eggs.

"Good point, Georgi. And what if I decide to finally start training for an Ironman? It *could* happen." I quickly nudged the eggs, hash browns, chorizo, and who knows what all back together on my plate. They looked a *lot* happier. "So, you started playing with the Illinois-Wisconsin stuff, and … what?"

"I walked back through the crime scenes." He put his fork down, inclining that perfect upper body over my counter. "I figured this has to be one of those either/or kinds of cases, right?"

I leaned back and narrowed my eyes at him, giving him the benefit of the doubt with a head nod.

"If this *is* some kind of redneck nightmare going around picking off hapless Illinoisans for no other reason than that they live in the wrong zip code, then he's going to be the kind of guy that goes for symbolism, right?"

"Yeah, probably." I sipped my coffee. It needed a warm-up.

"And it stands to reason a guy like that, if he really were from Wisconsin, he'd know he'd just buried a man neck-deep in the middle of a sacred Indian burial ground, right?"

"Native American effigy mound." Georgi corrected.

I chuckled. "Yeah, so?"

"So, why would he do that? What is he trying to tell us?" He got up, grabbed my mug, and topped it off.

I shrugged my shoulders. "Maybe 'I hate Natives'?'" I took the steaming mug of coffee he handed me. "Thanks."

Georgi put her hand over her mug. "I'm good."

"But the vic wasn't Native." Nick put the coffee pot back and grabbed a file from the top of the refrigerator before taking his seat on the stool. He placed an aerial photo of the golf course in front of us. I could make out what looked like chalk markings outlining burial mounds on one hole.

Nick drew a finger over the longest chalk marking on the photo. "Or maybe he's getting cleverer and wants us to join him for the next round of Scrabble. Winner takes all."

"Cut the mystery, Nick. You're killing me." I couldn't keep the timbre of annoyance out of my voice.

He stepped around to my side and leaned in, towering over the photo and me. Warmth flickered between us. He moved the photo a few degrees. "See anything out of place?"

I studied the photo, starting with the time-and-date stamp on the side. "Oh. It's fresh. From yesterday." My face flushed and my ribs tightened. I didn't know what I wasn't seeing. But I knew it couldn't be good. "I'm sorry, Georgi. I have a feeling you're not going to want to be around us for the next hour or so."

"Don't worry about it, sweetie. Cliff just texted, offering to pick me up. He wants to see if the Amish family at the farmers' market has any asparagus yet. In the meantime, I want to check out the woods, see if the morels are starting to show." She slid off her stool, placed her hand over mine, and squeezed it. "Call me when you can?"

"Of course. Good luck with the Amish asparagus."

She blew a kiss to Nick, gathered her things and left.

Returning my focus to the photo, I willed myself to see the same photo through a new lens. The white chalk rimming the burial mound faded to a dotted line near the spot where I'd made my gruesome discovery. But instead of the dead man's capped head and body, jagged marks and dark earth spilled over the ground. "Footprints in the chalk lines? It'll be impossible to tell if it was the bad guy or our guys at this point." I looked up at Nick.

"Right."

I stared down at the photo, following the long, slender chalk line with my finger. The tubular shape represented one of the thunderbird's wings. His round head and triangular body were purported to be within the mound itself, with the other wing spanning out underneath a row of viburnum bushes, out of sight. "I'm not seeing anything new."

"What about that wing tip?" Nick's index finger tapped the end of the thunderbird's wing.

I stopped forcing my eyes to consider what lay beneath the ground and instead gazed down at what *was* visible. The graceful wing shape, tapering to a sleek point. "Still nothing new here, Nick."

"Are you sure? Keep looking." Nick folded his arms.

A tingling sensation ran up my spine, and dark spots swam within the corners of my vision. "Is there a point to the wing tip? Is it pointing somewhere …?" My voice faded as ants crawled up the back of my throat.

"I got this picture from a friend of mine. The minute Quinn invited me in on this case, I decided to do all I could to assist. You know, get the Bureau back in his good graces."

"So, you just happened to know a guy who owed you a favor? Enough of a favor that he took a bird up early this morning and took some flyover shots?" The significance of this maneuver fell over me like a shroud. Nick wouldn't make such an extravagant gesture without reason. How had he known the killer's message might be best seen from above? Was it a message? Or was it Nick's protective hormones on steroids?

"Around five thirty this morning, I had a hunch, and I'm pretty sure it's turning out to be awfully important."

The shroud turned into steel, pressing me up against the wall, squeezing the air from my lungs.

"The course isn't open, Jo. No one else was there. Our guy had to have picked the location intentionally." Nick shifted his weight. He was right. Nick was on to something with the wingspan. Something horrible.

"It looks like the wing tip is pointing to my lot." My voice was flat, lifeless.

"Yeah. Heckuva clue." He shook his head.

"So, what's he telling us? I'm the next victim? Or he's inviting us to play with him?"

"One of the two."

"But I'm not from Illinois."

"You live there now."

I groaned. "You don't know it's pointing to anything. Could just be ..." I didn't want to say it out loud. We didn't believe in them. No one in law enforcement really does.

He pushed the aerial photo directly in front of me. "A coincidence?" His face was a dark mask. "It's not. The only thing we know for sure is he knew what he was doing when he chose this spot." Anger tinged his words. "And that means he was either going for the symbolism of the burial mound—or he knows you own that lot, and he has some kind of connection to *you*." His jaw ticked.

I traced the top of the white chalk outline, back and forth, pulled my index finger through the wing span, tapping on the tip. Then I moved my eyes toward the edge of the fairway, beyond a stand of scrub brush, up the little cart path leading directly onto my lot.

"What rang your bells in this direction?" I asked. "What makes you think the killer knows me?"

Nick gave a half smile. "It's too neat, Jo. While I admit it's not a hundred percent, why pick the effigy mound that basically leads the way to your lot?"

"It might be the mound itself, the animal itself. Maybe the wings are less about directing your attention to me and more about the symbolism thing." I wanted to comfort him and was pretty sure I was failing. "There aren't any connections between me and the other vics, are there?"

Nick shook his head. "I'm willing to set that angle aside for a moment—"

I stepped into his space and kissed him. "Thank you."

CHAPTER TWELVE

When we separated ourselves from each other again, he said, "I'm hoping I can lure you out of your R and R for a little work on the side. You can be my consultant."

"*Your* consultant? What about Quinn?"

Nick shrugged. I wasn't going to go there.

"Can I assume you've shared the kill-site coordinates with your big-city buddies?" I pushed my stool away from the counter, stood up and stretched, arms clasped over my head.

Nick watched me like a hungry lion at feeding time. "Yes. I've got the map." "Pull it up. Let's take a look." I had no doubt the murder map would be much easier to decipher than any scattergram charting the trajectory of our relationship. "Show me something I can understand."

He offered me a half smile, but his eyes seemed sad. "Check it out. Four locales, four black stars. Dates and approximate times of death posted in white font within." He turned the laptop toward me.

"Government issue?" The screen revealed a detailed topography map. I clicked on the first star. The black-and-white photo obscured the ice-covered lake. The dead man's body rested on the ice. From this angle, it'd be easy to think he'd been decapitated, if you didn't know his head was submerged in a little round ice-fishing hole.

"Keep going."

I clicked on the next star. The scene in Westfield off Highway 51 appeared. The viciously beaten body hidden in a snowy field wouldn't have been visible without the yellow outline. "Am I looking at these in order?"

"Yes. Nothing's jumped out at me so far." Nick hit the right arrow button to the third scene.

A magnified view of the top of the bluff on Pigtail Alley, just off Highway 33, appeared. I could see the eyeliner of the dancer on a billboard advertising a gentlemen's club alongside the road. The body lay sprawled in a clearing, thick yellow highlighter outlining its shape. "There's got to be something more that connects each of these scenes."

Nick raised an eyebrow, waiting.

Lost in thought, I scrolled back to the shot of my dead golfer's head, outlined in yellow, connected to an approximation of where his body lay hidden in the sacred earth.

I sat there, leaning into the screen while Nick leaned into me. The inside of his arm brushed against me. Fire tore through my nerve endings. *Control yourself, woman.*

"Crandon, Westfield, Portage, Baraboo. What's he trying to tell us?" I channeled Mickey Spillane in the hopes it would calm my tone. I studied the map. "Let's check the distance between each point, see if there's any symmetry to consider. Was that one of the points you covered in the profiling class you taught?"

"Yes. I'll find it." Sitting down beside me, he pulled out his phone and started reading. "First site to second site, Crandon to Westfield. Where is it? Okay … looks like two-and-a-half hours, 151 miles, give or take."

"And Westfield to Portage, that's what, about half an hour?" I'd driven that road many times between Stevens Point and Baraboo during my undergrad days.

"Good memory. Twenty-eight minutes, about twenty-five miles." He kept thumbing through images on the tiny screen.

Memories of long ago evening rides under the stars floated into mind. Nick and I used to zip along back roads on his

Harley after working a long shift in Chicago, making it to Wisconsin before the bars closed, looking for a safe place to land. Together.

I pushed the memories away. "And Portage to Baraboo is twenty minutes, tops, probably the same number of miles." My voice was thick with regret.

"Yeah, more or less. And while there's a hint of a line for the first three sites, the Portage-Baraboo location cuts that theory short with a jig and a jag on the map." He tapped both dots with his forefinger.

"Sure. But just for the fun of it, let's say there *is* something here." I pulled out a tattered notebook from the kitchen junk drawer and returned to my stool. I drew the mitten-shaped map of Wisconsin on the last coffee-stained sheet of paper. "Makes me proud of my public-school education."

Nick rolled his eyes and then got up to freshen his coffee while watching my inner artist emerge.

I waved him away from my lukewarm mug and added the names of the towns nearest where each victim was found on my makeshift map. "It's not quite a straight line, but the kills do sort of come down to the point of a Y on the map."

Nick studied my work. "I'm not seeing your Y, but I *am* seeing a clear pattern." The dark tone of his voice gave me pause.

"Nick?"

He sat on the stool, staring off into space for several seconds. The color drained from his handsome face. When he finally spoke, he sounded like a drunk man. "Write in the mileage between each scene, please."

I cocked my head at him, raised a brow and did exactly that.

He stared at the map without speaking. Months away from Nick had done nothing to dull my appreciation for his numerous skills, public and private. One of his better-known public skills had always been that of a teacher. Private too, come to think of it, if any of the rumors were true.

I breathed in, held it for ten seconds and let it out, counting to ten again. It helped. *I think.* My heartbeat slowed, and I turned to face him. "You're thinking about what you taught in your profiling class in Mad Town?"

"Yes." He rubbed his knuckles across his lower lip. "A pattern theory."

"Woo-woo," I teased. Some of Nick's theories were pretty far out there. But today he didn't smile at my teasing. I cleared my throat.

"So, given your pattern theory, is there anything that might lead us in the direction of what he might be thinking of next?"

"Well, there are a couple of possibilities. The close association of the last two kills could mean that he's about to change his tack, move off his current trajectory and create a new one." Nick looked from the computer screen to my handwritten map. "Or, he could be going to ground, ready to hibernate for a season. But that doesn't feel right."

"Why not?"

"This feels more like anger than getting ready to set up camp and hide out to me." He commandeered his computer, punching in FBI passcodes.

"And if you're right, if he's changing tack, ramping it up, we'll see more kill sites. And you think they're going to follow a pattern similar to the kills we've seen so far, right?" I thought about this for a minute, then I drew a big arrow in a downward slash to the right of the crime-scene locations. "Which means, we could see a slew of new murders following a similar trajectory elsewhere in the state, correct?" I drew an up arrow on the left-hand side of the paper.

"It's possible. And one way of predicting next moves might be to get a range of possible locations within maybe a hundred-mile radius of Baraboo but headed up toward the Reedsburg–

LaValle area." Nick's face brightened. What did he know that I didn't?

"How is that good news for us at this point?" I was fishing. Why had he gone from desperado to yogi-like? What was going on in that mind of his?

"Well, I wouldn't call it good news. But I would say he's showing signs of classic decompensation—which may make him prone to errors." He ran his tongue inside his cheek.

"But how many bodies does it take for a killer to decompensate enough to catch?" I added the letters we'd found at the crime scenes to the small paragraph of information we were amassing on each murder. If we were going to start adding more letters, I was going to need more paper.

The brutal truth of a killer on the loose in my home state clubbed me over the head like a sack of rocks. I gripped the edge of the counter. Less than twenty-four hours ago, I was happily chopping through the rough, hunting for a lost golf ball. Four dead bodies, a touchy country sheriff, and one unpredictable quasi-boyfriend later—nothing in my life felt safe anymore.

Nick stretched one of his perfectly muscled legs to the floor, then came to stand behind me, massaging my neck and shoulders. The intimacy of the gesture threatened to awaken more of me than I was ready to offer. Sucking in air, I closed my eyes, steadying myself.

His gentle finger tracing across the back of my neck startled me into stillness. I opened my eyes and looked up just as he moved to lean against the counter beside me.

"Josie." He cupped my face in his hands and kissed the top of my head. He had a tiny dark cross etched on the inside of his right wrist. "Will you pray with me?" He dropped his hands down, placing my hand between both of his.

I bowed my head and closed my eyes.

"Father God, we come to you, asking that you grant us your supernatural ability to stop this killer. We need your help. Thank you for bringing me back into Josie's life, and we ask your guidance over what happens next between us." Nick ended his prayer with a squeeze of my hand.

"So now what?" I smiled, relieved.

His simple act of prayer had cleared the tension between us. *Funny how that happens. Bring something into the light, and things go from fuzzy to crystal clear pretty quickly.*

Nick shoved his phone back into his pocket. "Time to take this party on the road."

"Where are we going?" Why was I being included? That may have been a better question.

"We've got work to do. On different ends of the same rainbow." His eyes were bright.

Tremors of confusion rippled through me. "I thought we were all over your pattern idea?"

"Yes, we are. But we need to look at them from different angles. And you've already hit on my number one priority, and reminded me of a better way to utilize your hick expertise in your official capacity as my area consultant." He pulled his jacket on.

"I have?"

"Yes, you reminded me about my woo-woo class in Madison." He lowered his sunglasses over his face.

"Son of a sea biscuit," I said. "Are you thinking about the possibility of someone in your class becoming overly fond of your woo-woo theories and deciding to go for a little extra credit?"

His face was a grim mask. He nodded at me as he cleared our breakfast dishes. "Go get dressed, and bring your mitten-map."

CHAPTER THIRTEEN

"Where we going?" Ideas swam through my mind, triggered by Nick's classroom-connection theory.

"Back to school." He wound his way through the pine-tree-lined drive and headed down the gravel path that led to Snake Hill Road.

We arrived at the corner of Ski Hi Road and Highway 12 eight minutes later. I flicked my thumb to the left. "Turn and burn, baby. I'd like to see what this thing can do if you open her up once you hit the highway." Nick had never been a car guy until he drove a Tesla in a police impound lot and bought it from an officer of the court a week later.

He shook his head and turned onto the highway, pushing the sedan over seventy and holding steady. "Just enough of a touch to put us at the head of the class, not enough to be detained by the locals." He pulled out his cell phone and tossed it in my lap. "Amelia wants us to drop by the field office. Call Quinn?"

I nodded and found his name in Nick's contact list. Amelia Dixon was one of my favorite special agents. The Tesla's console lit up as the ringing filled the car. It clicked into voice mail in three rings. I looked over at my partner and left a message. "Quinn, Nick and I are heading to Madison on a lead. C'mon down the minute you get this. We'll be at the Bureau on State Street. Thanks." I ended the call.

"Feel that hot to you?" Nick's question surprised me.

"Yes. It absolutely does." I hadn't recognized the feeling until he'd asked about it. The tingling from earlier in the day had grown to a roar, and everything I had in me was hoping for a break. "The map, you suddenly teaching someone else's class and using your pet patterning theory. It all adds up to the possibility of a bad guy sitting in your class. The more I turn it around in my mind, the better it fits."

He nodded, two-handing the wheel. He pulled out into the oncoming lane and smoothly passed a semi with a double trailer, followed by a Camaro and a minivan. My kind of guy.

"I'm going through names and faces, and I've got two likelies. Both male. One looks pretty good for it, and one looks even better." He tapped on the steering wheel as if communicating in Morse code.

"Tell me all about Even Better Guy first." I was struck by how good it felt to be next to him, driving in a squad together again, barreling into the middle of a case. *I was born for this. We were born for this.*

"Alex Burdock. Sits in the front row. Wears stripes with plaids, expensive loafers, and bow ties."

"Since when does being a fashionista make a guy a criminal?" A smile crept across my face.

"It's more than just his fashion sense. He has the eyes. And he's careful, interested in the material, practically sits at my feet, yet he's buttoned-up. He feels forced, studied. Plus, what's a guy like that need me for? He's a high school guidance counselor." Nick seemed to be taking his measure, but did he have enough information to start a profile on Burdock?

"And your number two?"

"Second guy's just creepy. And angry. Could be a deadly combination." He slowed to accommodate the curves of a traffic circle.

"Frickin' roundabouts." I tsked loudly.

Nick shook his head.

"What? This ain't England." The base of my neck tightened.

"They're efficient."

"And cost more than, what, a million bucks a pop? Don't get me started."

"Deal. Back to the case. Something we have the potential to solve. You asked about my second-in-line."

"Fine. Name? Background?" Impatience coursed through me.

"He's got a vanilla name. Smith or Jones-esque. But he's definitely the kind of guy you might never forget under the right circumstances."

I shivered. That was my least favorite kind of killer.

Nick thumped his hand on the wheel. "White. His name's Melvin White. Knew it was imminently forgettable."

"Name like Melvin, you're pretty much destined for a life of crime."

"The thing with him is how completely unremarkable, uncriminal, he is. Guy's got a public library card for Pete's sake."

"And you know this because?"

"Because he leaves a book out on his desk in every class. Spine pointed in my direction, I can't help but read it." His voice slowed with every word. "Almost as if he wanted me to see them."

"Oh no. So, can you think of any titles?" Any number of clues could be hidden in a perp's habits.

"True crime. They were all true crime. Some of the grittiest."

"Crap." I pushed my sunglasses up and rubbed my eyes with my thumb and forefinger.

"Yeah. Text it in for me, would you please?" He nodded toward his phone.

I plucked it from the console and sent texts with the names of each man to Amelia. She responded with three icons: a thumbs up, a red heart, and a smacking set of red lips. I rolled my eyes. *Nice. Glad to see Nick is still keeping it strictly professional with his coworkers.*

"Done. Remind me, you've been teaching your geo woo-woo class in Madison for … how long?"

"Almost six weeks." He passed a white pickup, a fallen-soldier decal prominently displayed on the back of the cab, nodding at the baseball-capped driver as we passed. The driver nodded back.

"And your class is made up of mostly law-enforcement types?"

"Mostly." His eyes bounced among all three mirrors at equal intervals. He should be teaching defensive driving. Come to think of it, he did.

"So …" I didn't want to even think about dealing with a dirty cop again.

"Maybe. Maybe not. Not everyone's law enforcement." Was he reading my mind?

"Who's *not everyone*, pray tell?" I had a feeling he might be talking about our top two.

"Tweedle Dee and Tweedle Dum are not everyone. One's a high school guidance counselor like I said, and one owns a convenience store." He'd done his homework on his class roster. That didn't surprise me.

"Holy cow. I've never heard of a killer high school guidance counselor. Puts a whole new spin on those aptitude tests though, doesn't it?"

He smirked and pushed the car up to just a hair under eighty miles per hour.

We rode along in silence, the specter of a serial killer posing as one of Nick's students sitting heavy between us. The rolling countryside lulled me into distant memories. Each one featured Nick prominently.

"Cat got your tongue, Josie?" His voice pulled me out of my reverie.

"Are we going to talk about it?" I choked out the words.

"*It* meaning us?" He raised a brow and glanced at me longer than street legal as he drove.

Steam rollers pushed up my throat. My anguished silence filled the air between us.

He pulled into a wayside stop and parked under an old oak. "We've got a head start on Quinn. We can afford a few minutes in the shade. Time for a badly needed talk." Unbuckling his seat belt, he turned to me, sliding one hand through my hair. "Am I starting? Or are you?"

I closed my eyes. *Use your words, Josie.* "I ..." I put my hand over his, pulled it down into my lap, cradled it. "When I ... the time I was in the hospital ... when you ..." *Gah! C'mon, woman up.* "I was afraid. I wasn't ready. Or I thought I wasn't. But then I was. And by then, you were gone."

His eyes glistened, and his face turned from empathic to ... embarrassed? "Not a day goes by that's not soaked with regret for what I did."

Great. He thinks I'm blaming him. "But it was me too. I kept pushing you away. I *asked* you to leave. It was just ... when you didn't come back, I was afraid you gave up on me."

"I should never have left your side." His right hand wrenched free from my grasp, and he raked it through his hair. "When I *did* come back to see you before you left the hospital ... after Kira ... and you refused to see me, I should've tried harder. Should've ignored your words. Should've known it was the painkillers talking. Not you."

"No. You don't get to do that. Don't you dare put that on yourself. You don't think I've been swimming in regret ever since I pushed you away?" Hot tears trickled down my cheeks. "I have to live with knowing what this has done to you. To Sam. Even from a million miles away." I willed myself to stop the tears.

"You weren't yourself. You were heavily sedated. You'd been wounded. I shouldn't have listened to a word you said that day. I knew better." Agony laced his tone. "And then the time stretched on, and I was too ashamed of walking away to face you again. But I couldn't just let Sam be."

Sam. I needed to tell him about what Kira had done now. His pain, the unfairness of it, tore through me. "That's just not right. I knew exactly what I was saying, and it wasn't the first time you'd heard it from me. If anything, your foresight and your Leatherman, saved my life that day."

"*You* saved your own life that day. Your strength, your will to live, your courage." He wiped at his eye.

"You did the right thing." I softened my tone, hoping to send forgiveness and love his way. But he needed to hear my words. I sniffled.

He shook his head. "You stuck that knife into Kira and saved yourself and countless other potential victims that day. And your brave actions put a killer behind bars. You brought closure to families. That had nothing to do with me."

"I forgive you, Nick—even though there's nothing to forgive, I forgive you. And I'm asking you to do the same for me. Can you forgive me for pushing you away all this time?"

He cupped his right hand over my cheek. His eyes were a mystery to me. "I adore you, Jo Oliver. And I already forgave you. I just couldn't forgive myself."

"Kira's not through with us yet, Nick."

"What do you mean?"

"It's Sam—somehow Kira's used her connections to throw a wrench in the adoption."

He gripped the wheel. "What do you mean, a wrench?"

"I don't know yet. I just got a letter a few days ago. They've put it on hold to assess my mental health or something. Who knows what she—"

Fog lifted in my brain. *I couldn't just let Sam be.* I narrowed my eyes at him. "What did you say earlier? About Sam?"

He took a deep breath. Let it out. "Sam needed us. Needs us. I couldn't just walk away from her, couldn't just be another nameless, shapeless father figure shoving off in the night. I went to see her, Jo. I'm sorry I didn't tell you, but I went to see her. To let her know she can count on me. No matter what." He spread his hands out wide, pressing them into his thighs.

He'd gone behind my back to see Sam. He'd gone above and beyond not to abandon a little girl, no matter the cost. He'd done the right thing—even if I wasn't ready to admit it. I sighed, gathered his hands up into mine. "Can we drop this for a while? Can we get back to being partners again? Can't we just be okay together?"

"Yeah. Sure. Back to the case." He returned to the wheel, buckled himself in, and steered the car out onto the highway.

CHAPTER FOURTEEN

Nick pulled into an unmarked parking spot. He looked over at me, resting his eyes on mine. I drank him in, waves of sorrow pounding under his cloud of pride. Sorrow I had brought into his life.

I threw a mini prayer to God. *Father, I can't fix this. Please restore whatever it is we're meant to be to each other. Make a way in the wilderness. Your will. Our lives. Amen.*

"What are you looking at, handsome? Let's go speak a little Feebaneese, shall we?" I winked at him, hoping to evoke the bravado of our youth. Back in the day when we thought there was nothing cooler than being a member of the FBI. We thought they'd have their own language, their own culture. We were right.

"You know the drill, beautiful. My world, my rules." He slid out of the car, and I did the same. We reached the entrance together. He snuck a kiss. *Smooth.*

"You think they'll let me in?" I put my arm through his.

"Better stay nice and close." He leaned into me, opened the door and led the way. He breezed past the security booth and waved me toward a pair of agents tasked with screening the visitors.

I endured the security check, relieved to see Special Agent Dixon waiting patiently for us at the edge of the rotunda, several feet down the hallway. I hugged the slender blonde. "So great to see you, Amelia. You look amazing."

"Right back at you. I wish we could've had a chance to catch up under better circumstances." She nodded at Nick. "How you doing, hot stuff?"

He rolled his eyes with a slight shake of his head. "What, no hug for me? Isn't that some sort of discrimination?"

"Not while your wildcat Josie's in the house. If you're asking me to put my life on the line for a hug from a hot special agent, I'm taking a rain check." She winked at me and turned to lead us to a bank of elevators.

We crossed a marble floor emblazoned with the FBI crest. The rotunda was lined with busts and plaques of well-known special agents along with descriptions of their heroism. I loved walking through this building. It was a combination history lesson and patriotism booster shot all in one. These men and women risked their lives daily to keep our country safe. I never tired of learning more about them, past and present. We reached the elevator, and Amelia punched the top-floor button.

"Amelia?" Nick turned to her with wide eyes and an upturned hand. "Your mystery text brought me to you in record time. What's up?"

She looked at us in confusion for a few seconds. "I see no one's told you." A dark expression turned her features into a cold mask.

The elevator opened into a huge expanse of a room that covered the entire floor of the building. Special Agent Dixon led Nick and me through a maze of cubicles into a glass-walled conference room at the center of the floor. Thick windows framed with equally thick steel bars screamed "bulletproof" even from here.

Inside, two Brooks Brothers–suited men were at the table, poring over laptops. They started to get to their feet as we entered.

"At ease, boys. These are friendlies." Amelia waved them back down with one hand. With her girl-next-door good looks and cheerleader figure, it'd be easy to forget she was in charge of this operation. And it'd be a mistake.

"Hector, show us what you've got." Amelia nodded toward the ceiling, and one of the men poked a button on a remote, releasing a large screen. She made the introductions as her agents set up shop.

"I take it you've got bad news for us?" Impatience was my strong suit.

"In a minute." Amelia's tone grew cooler.

"Where would you like us?" I smiled at her. *You go, girl.*

"How about you two sit here? You'll have a great view of both the screen and our computers."

I nudged Nick and sat down as directed. I could practically feel his irritation. I pulled out the chair next to mine and patted it. *When in Rome ...*

Amelia waited, patient as a school marm, for Nick to sit down. "Okay, we know we had four male victims, from four different parts of Illinois, found in four different parts of Wisconsin."

Hector handed her the remote. Pictures of each crime scene filled the screen. Even though I knew what to expect, there was always something I just couldn't stomach about seeing crimes larger than life. No matter how many crime scenes I saw, my mind floated to their families, to their worlds, to the tragedy of a life cut short.

Compassion mixed with anger fueled my investigations—sometimes interfering with my professionalism. It's what *wouldn't* have made me a good special agent. It's what also made me a great small town police chief.

Nick remained silent. Silence agreed with him.

"And what we know of the cause of death so far would not have linked these crimes together. As we all know, weapons matter. But if the killer's message involves his choice of weapon, we haven't cracked it yet." She showed a picture of the icy hole and continued. "So far, we have a drowning, a beating, a long-distance rifle, and a man poisoned and buried up to his neck on a golf course. Each crime unique until now."

Nick and I exchanged a glance. He forged ahead, honing in on the other important detail. "Until now?"

Amelia grimaced and nodded. Then, she hit the button to forward to another picture, one I'd never seen before. "Now we've got a fifth victim."

I wheeled my chair away from the table to face the screen, landing me close enough to nudge Nick's thigh with my own. His nearness comforted me. I relaxed my shoulders, stretched out my neck and tightened and released my toes before looking up at the screen.

A long, lithe body was draped like a ragdoll, face down, across a wooden sign. It was bent at the waist, curly dark hair and dangling arms obscuring the sign's white lettering. The grotesque diorama laid out on the screen above was one that I'd never be able to erase from my head. *Ugh. I hate this part of the job.*

Nick snapped into his professional-recorder mode. "What's the body draped over, a Welcome to Reedsburg sign?"

Special Agent Dixon nodded slowly.

"Is that a male or a female?"

I'd been wondering the same thing in the more cognizant regions of my brain.

"Male, like the others. Thirty-six years old. Youngest victim so far. Tourist. No connections to the other victims, yet." Dixon referred to her notes. "Kyle. Kyle Wirth. His cousin's a fourth-generation pig farmer, just took over the family operation last fall. Divorced. Two young children. Says Kyle visited every year right about now."

"Cause of death?" Nick's thigh pressed against mine. *I'm here for you, girl.*

I noted a tremor in his leg. What was he seeing? "This connects to one of your theories, doesn't it?" I asked.

His leg fell away. "Maybe. Cause of death, Special Agent?"

Dixon glanced at us, puzzled. Was she trying to figure out who we were to each other now? *Join the club.* She looked back down at her notes. "Also poisoned, but it's the combination that interested me. The results aren't official yet, but we're pretty sure he was poisoned with chemicals common to his cousin's pig-farming operation."

"You'll remember me." Nick's voice was trancelike.

"That's what the killer's telling us?" I translated in an instant. Eerie as it was, it felt good to be on the trail together.

"He's getting bolder, but it's more than bold. He's telling us he's above us. Untouchable." Nick's definite tone told me he was connecting the dots.

I turned to Amelia. "You're certain this is the work of the same man?"

"Or woman."

A light switched on. I turned to Amelia. "You said the vic's a tourist? Like the others? From Illinois?"

Amelia shook her head. "That's the oddity. This victim is from upstate New York."

"Shoots our rivalry theory in the head." I scowled. *Now what?* I stared at the screen, signature letters from each scene floating over each star on the map overhead.

"Speaking of letters, was there a letter left at this scene as well?" I had no idea what to make of the string of letters so far. Maybe another would be the key.

The two agents seated across the table from us came alive. Hector was the designated spokesman. "We have unofficial confirmation of a white bead with a capital letter *A* found in the victim's pocket."

"*A?*" *What the heck?* Impatience stomped on my nerves. I wanted to ask the difference between *unofficial* and *official* confirmation, but I let it slide. *Who says you can't teach an old girl new tricks?*

I mentally reviewed the letters found so far: *J, E, ME, H,* and now *A*. Was it a name? An organization? An anagram? I came up with exactly … nothing.

Hector looked up from his laptop. "Special Agent Dixon, you'll want to see this."

She frowned at her colleagues. "Put it up on the screen."

"Yes, ma'am." Hector's fingers clicked the mouse at warp speed.

Several seconds later, a screen containing the death photos of all five men stared down at us. The room was quiet as we studied the faces. Listless fidgeting telegraphed when most of us reached the photo of the last victim. A bolt of lightning could not have made things any clearer. I turned to Nick, scanning his fine features, olive skin, thick black hair, knowing that Amelia and the other two agents in the room were following my lead.

Hector's twin broke the ice. "Is it just my imagination, or do these guys look eerily similar? Think it's just the camera angle, or the lighting or something?"

I didn't break eye contact with Nick. "No. It's not your imagination. It's the color of their skin, the thickness of their wavy black hair." I reached out to touch Nick's close-cropped, ebony hair. "They look just like you."

CHAPTER FIFTEEN

"You can't go on hair color and skin tone and say you've got a pattern," Nick objected. "Half the men in this state would look identical with such meager information." Nick's face was a mask, but I could sense his anger. And embarrassment.

"Right," I said, "but when you add the same eye color and relatively same build, you've got to take it seriously. Nick, this could be it. Your class could have been his trigger. Now's the time to tell them what you're thinking."

"Let's talk about your class, Nick." Amelia sat and rested her elbows on the table. "You gave us the names of two students you thought we should check out. Why don't you fill us in?" The special agents in the room were silent, all eyes on Nick.

Things were breaking fast if this *was* a break. The FBI's proverbial left hand hadn't had time to inform the right hand of what had popped. The way my own neurons were firing, this had to be a break, or I'd have to turn in my shield. My inner horsepower strained against the bit, willing me to loosen the reins and let them have their head … and run into the hunt.

Nick put his phone on the table and stood up. "I'm teaching a profiling course through UW-Madison, as an adjunct. Less than an adjunct really, I'm a substitute. This was retired Special Agent Chase Lafferty's course, and I was tapped to step in when he died."

Nick looked into the middle distance, over Amelia's left shoulder. The strain of rehashing events had etched a deep line across his brow. "Lafferty had an established curriculum.

When I was tapped to fill in for him, I was encouraged to put my own spin on the class."

Amelia shifted her weight from one pump to another and stared at him. "So, you took that as an invitation to share your own theories?"

I didn't like her tone, or what she was implying. Sure, I called it Nick's woo-woo theory, but that didn't mean I didn't respect it. Or him. She was playing dirty. Or it might've been my personal bias. I kept my hand on Nick's thigh and my mouth shut.

"Yes." Thick cables of muscle tightened under my hand. A hint of red appeared on Nick's cheek.

"Enlighten me. Take it from the top. What exactly did you teach that class?"

Nick pulled in air, puffed out his cheeks and started jiggling his leg. I raised my hand off his leg and put it in my lap.

Nick formed a *V* with the index and second finger of his right hand and held it up. "I used this exact pattern as an example in class." He snapped into teacher-mode. "Drop your smart board and pull up a map of Wisconsin, and I'll show you." He moved from teacher to bossy-mode. A step up.

Amelia complied.

Nick walked over to the smart board and grabbed a remote pen off the conference table. "I showed a large map of Wisconsin to the class. Then I picked out a spot from the northeast corner of the state and drew a dot. No name, not a real village or city, just a dot." He demonstrated by drawing a dot on the map with the special marker.

"Okay." Amelia must've known what was coming. Her eyes traveled down to where the next dot would soon be added.

"Then I drew another dot, arbitrarily, a way down from the first one." He marked another dot. "And then I drew a third one, maybe half the distance between the first two." He filled in a third dot. "And at half the distance between the third and the second dot, I drew a fourth dot, right about here." He marked a fourth dot on the smart board. "And I basically explained that while every killer has his or her own motivation for doing what they do, they often fall into recognizable patterns. And it's the pattern that can lead us to the killer. I walked them through how to search for patterns. The *Y* pattern was just an example."

"A little-known example taken from Quantico materials, though, if memory serves." Amelia read my mind.

"I don't know anymore. All I can tell you is I'd thrown a bunch of dots up to represent kill spots and told my students to imagine the mind of an organized killer who had a sense of symmetry and balance to his kills. I just spontaneously decided to use a letter of the alphabet as my organizing graphic—to illustrate my point. I connected the dots to show them how the kill spots could form the letter *Y* if you looked at the spots on a map. The whole point of the exercise was to help students think differently about a set of data points during an investigation, to help them start seeing patterns." He set the marker on the table, waiting for Amelia to respond.

A snowplow of emotion slammed into me. The undeniable way in which his theoretical dots corresponded with actual murder sites hit me like two tons of slush. Beads of sweat broke out across my forehead.

Dixon's face was white. "And if you were to put the murder sites in red on that map?" She plucked a red marker off the table and handed it to him.

Nick carefully underlined the names of the cities closest to the four murder sites on the map before us. They were nearly identical. His hands were steady. I was proud of him.

An idea snaked through me. "Profilers all over the country use similar theories to track their killers. Aren't there a host of famous crimes easily accessible that would involve patterns of some sort?" I caught Nick's gaze and held it. "This killer could have chosen to pattern his crimes after any one of them."

Amelia cleared her throat. "Yes, duly noted, Chief."

Nick isn't going to bear the weight of this alone. Not if I can help it.

Nick averted his eyes. *Was he mad I jumped into the water to try to bring him to safety? One more awesome layer of complication settling between us.* His face was unreadable. "For each of the theoretical kill spots, I explained that all killers leave a signature, whether we discover it or not. It's as individual as a fingerprint, and it's what often leads to their capture."

"And the signature in your theoretical case ... it involved the relative travel time and distance between each crime scene?" Dixon knew the answer, but she wanted to draw him further out.

"Yes. And in my example, I had the class map out what a similar trajectory of murder sites might look like on the other side." Nick's voice was low.

"The other side?" Amelia was cross-examining him.

"Of the letter *Y.* I had them assume for this exercise the imaginary killer was mirroring his kill spots, using similar travel times and distances between crime scenes ... traveling up the other side of the *Y.*"

Amelia pressed a button on a small power strip on the table in front of her, and a map of Wisconsin filled the screen.

The first four murder scenes were represented by black stars, with the stats for each underneath the star. Just like the images from Nick's computer. A line snaked down the screen past the first four cities. It seemed to pause, forming a base between the Portage and Baraboo stars.

And then it started climbing back up the other side. The stats between the Reedsburg and Baraboo murders were an exact match to the time, date, and distance data points between the Baraboo and Portage murders.

I'd been in the business long enough to know that killers had distinct patterns and that cracking the puzzle was the quickest way to catch the killer. Once Nick shared with us the details of a simulation he'd taught in Madison, we were spellbound. The class assignment, randomly designed by Nick to demonstrate how a psychopath might create a mirror pattern, looked exactly like the map taking shape before our eyes. We were pretty close to convinced we were on the right trail.

We were in Nick's world now. I'd never heard of a killer operating based on some sort of murder map, but if Nick had used this exact example in class, his students were looking better and better for the crimes. Knowledge did nothing to stem the tide of nausea rolling over me. I closed my eyes, stretched my head up and took a long, deep breath, hoping against hope to get ahead of it.

I shook my head to clear it, opened my eyes and turned to look at Nick. "So, if this guy is from your class, he's taunting you? Showing you his homework?"

"Maybe. We can't discount the possibility." He tapped his finger on the arm of his chair, wondering out loud as much as answering my question.

"Well, I've never seen this before." Amelia put the marker down. "But I have seen killers mess with agents, Nick. And while this may somehow be connected to you, it's *not* your fault. The students you asked us to look into?"

"Burdock and White. Both were overly interested in the pattern. The minute I'd drawn the map of Wisconsin, it was as if they were the only two in the room for the rest of the hour."

"What do we know about them? Hector?"

"As we speak," he said, indicating he had agents looking into all of Nick's students.

"I want priority on these two."

I squeezed Nick's thigh, keeping my voice low. "Burdock stood out to you."

Nick let out a long breath. "He had a chip on his shoulder, that's for sure. He stayed after class every single session. And, more often than not, when he left would take something." He looked down. "Of mine."

"Like what?" I asked.

"My pen. My notebook. And once I'm almost sure he took my jacket. Just a few weeks ago, I reached out to him, left him an email telling him I'd heard he may have taken my jacket by mistake. The next day, I found it in my office, hanging from my chair."

"Did you call security?" Anger pressed in at the back of my neck.

"No, of course not. I wasn't sure I hadn't just left it there myself." Electricity swirled in the air around us.

"After that, I just kept everything as close to me as possible. I figured he had a man crush on me, and I didn't want to either embarrass or encourage him." Nick's eyes focused on the wall as he walked through his recent memory.

"And the last time he was in class, did he take anything?" Fire roared through my nerves.

"My black leather gloves."

The dull roar that had been sounding through my body reached my temples and turned the volume all the way up.

Hector was punching his cell phone furiously. "I'll see if they've turned up in evidence at any of the crime scenes."

I looked up at him. "If he does have your gloves, what's it mean?"

He sighed, rubbing his forehead. "So, when a psychopath fixates on a person, their goal is to own them, become them in a twisted way. They stalk their prey, obsessing about them, wanting to know what it feels like to live their life; feel what it feels to be in their skin."

"Like wearing your gloves?" A chill swept over me. "Or your coat?"

Silence filled the room. Amelia and Hector exchanged a glance. She shifted her weight. "It's definitely a bad sign if Burdock really is that far advanced, that into Nick."

An iceberg nestled in the pit of my stomach. "So, let's pick him up. Kick him around a little. Get to his house. Find the stupid gloves. Have you sent teams to check out his residence?"

The group's stares unnerved me. "Screw the legal requirement! Can't you send a team to just hang around, see if you can cook up a reason to get inside, look around?" My bias for action was stronger than ever.

Hector's phone lit up. He paused to read it aloud. "No gloves matching your description."

"At least they haven't been found at a crime scene." Nick shook his head. "Yet. It's probably going to happen, might as well be prepared."

CHAPTER SIXTEEN

After a five-minute break, now armed with bottles of water, we turned our attention to Hector while we waited for Amelia to return to the glass-box conference room.

His phone buzzed. He read a few texts and reached for the remote. "Check this out. Burdock's elementary and middle-school records show scores of contacts with counselors and deans. Most of them involve reports of bullying."

I looked at him. "Any descriptions of the alleged bullies?"

Hector pushed a button on the remote and scrolled through a half-dozen pages on the screen. He stopped at a picture of a smiling young man with black hair, brown eyes, and olive skin.

I was unable to stop myself from reading out loud. "Says here one Daniel Salvatore, one of Burdock's counselors from Camp Oshewan in Northern Wisconsin, resigned under unsubstantiated accusations of abuse. No further information available."

Goosebumps skittered over my arms. Daniel Salvatore looked a lot like a much younger version of Nick. "Burdock's abused by a camp counselor years ago, and then, what? Marches into class, spots Nick and places himself in victim mode, starts imagining the abuse all over again, with a bigger, badder, grown up version of Daniel Salvatore?"

"And he snaps!" Hector's voice sparked through the air. "But what about White? Is he involved?"

"They met in class, I'd swear to it." Nick's color returned as he spoke. "Either that or they're Academy Award–level actors. And trust me, they're not."

"Dare I ask what White looks like?" Dread spread over me like a shadow.

"Ugh." Hector texted. "You don't want to know." But he put the man's picture on the screen. Just like the others.

"Crap. So vic number, what? Six, will turn out to be Burdock's classmate?" In my mind's eye, I could see agents running in all directions at once. Where would I be sent?

The door opened and Amelia stepped back into the room. "We've got teams heading to last known addresses for both White and Burdock."

"Great." Now, something about Camp Oshewan was swimming around in the back of my mind.

Amelia started scribbling on the whiteboard. "Melvin White. Last known addresses include both Waupon and Portage, rents a one-bedroom apartment in each town. He's not exactly a pillar of either community. Co-owns a barely-legal puppy mill in one and is suspected of running dog fights in the other. Teams should be on site in about ten more minutes."

She looked away from the whiteboard, staring over our heads for a fraction of a second longer than I was comfortable. Then she snapped her head back to center, shiny-eyed, muscles twitching under her alabaster skin. "Mr. White is a person of extreme interest. He has a rather significant history of mental illness. Variety of run-ins with the law from an early age. Juvenile record includes violent outbursts and, I quote, 'featuring uncontrollable fits of rage.'"

"Wow. Reads like a serial-killer résumé." How'd they miss all this on the background check for the profiler class? What had the guy been doing in the front row of Nick's back-to-school nights? "He got more than one identity maybe?"

Amelia nodded slowly. "Apparently, our Mr. White spent the greater part of his youth in an Amish colony in Wisconsin."

"Amish?" I leaned forward in my seat. "There is a significant Amish presence near Camp Oshewan, where Burdock was abused. White and Burdock *have* to be working together. Way too many connections popping up for this to be random."

"It's not enough," Nick said. "Why me? What led him to me or to Special Agent Lafferty before me? Maybe that's our connection." Nick must've shared my feeling of being one off on this case.

The tremor in Nick's fingers told me he was struggling too. I sighed. We were missing something. *Something big.* "Or maybe it was just dumb luck. Burdock walks into your class, sees you and BOOM! He regresses. Something's triggered. Sees White's true crime obsession, and cozies up to ol' Mel like bees to honey. If White has two identities, maybe he's using his Wisconsin persona to make it look like he's killing people from Illinois. Throwing us off the scent, when what he's really doing is playing out this victimization over and over again."

"But we have a New Yorker now." Nick was nodding slowly, lost in thought. "And there's only one way this can end."

I nodded. "Wait—what do you mean?"

"What if Burdock's become the ultimate bully? He's killing men that remind him of his abuser. Who triggered him?"

"*You* did. Oh crap." A medicine ball of realization slammed into my stomach.

Amelia scrolled down to another page of the report on her screen, brows knit together.

Hector's fingers flew over the keys. "We better see what else the boys have to tell us about my friend Burdock."

I nudged Nick. "So, White totes creepy library books to school. Attracts Burdock's attention. I can buy that connection, Burdock falls in love with you for aforementioned reasons."

Photos of Burdock and White appeared on the screen above me, side by side. "They could have been the original Mutt and Jeff. Says here Burdock is 5'10" to White's 6'3". Blond, blue-eyed beach boy with attitude meets lean, swarthy Mr. Average with a serious ax to grind."

Hector chuffed. "Yeah, and you might easily pass either of them on the street without a second thought."

I shivered. "Not me. Look at those eyes." White's physical dominance was no match for the evil glittering from Burdock's face.

"Burdock is a high school guidance counselor. From a western suburb in Du Page County." Nick said.

My curiosity danced out of a corner of my mind, landing front and center.

Amelia kept writing. "White is still my frontrunner. As Nick said, Burdock is currently living in Hinsdale and works at a private Catholic high school a few suburbs over. He's in his eleventh year there and is apparently a well-respected, tenured member of the faculty. Pretty sure there's a ground team at his house already."

I rolled my eyes. "Figures."

"What, him being a tenured faculty member? That figures for you?" Nick seemed genuinely curious.

"No. The plaids with stripes and the bowtie. Right up the Catholic schools' alley." I recalled my own brief stint as a Catholic school girl.

I'd been the smartest kid in my grade every year. Had it not been for the perfect storm of a cute Italian boy named Amado and a pack of cigarettes whirling through the halls when I was twelve years old, I'd probably still be a practicing Catholic. I looked over at Nick and smiled, wisely choosing to keep my reminiscing to myself. *Always have had a soft spot for cute Italian boys.*

I took a deep breath and invited in thoughts of ocean kayaking and gentle sea turtles until my head cleared and I was ready to return to the crazy stream of information on the screen. Refocusing my thoughts on Burdock's profile, I searched for anything that might help explain my theory.

Amelia's face turned beet red. "The man left articles of his own clothing specifically for you to find. Of course I'm going to have him thoroughly checked out." She was a mama bear if anyone got between her and the safety of one of her agents. And Nick was part of her FBI family. Messing with him was messing with one of her own.

Hector nodded. "This could matter."

Amelia's impatience swirled around her. "What?"

"Melvin White owned a small outfitters' shop in Wildcat Mountain. Is that a real place?" He stared at me.

"Yes. Sort of. Go on." It would take too long to explain the enchanting beauty of Wildcat Mountain to a city boy. Let alone the fact that anyone claiming to own a business "on Wildcat Mountain" typically owned one in Hillsboro. I let it slide.

Hector shrugged his shoulders. "Catered to hunters and river enthusiasts. Sold guns, crossbows, all kinds of knives. Rented out a few fishing boats, canoes, kayaks, and the occasional paddle board."

Amelia tapped the table. "And he has been known to frequent online dating sites."

I stared up at the olive-skinned faces of the five victims, willing one of them to reveal the puzzle to me. The image of my eldest cousin's online dating "stable" came to mind.

"We're looking into expedited subpoenas from the dating sites now."

"Thank God, no one's ever done that on *us*." I winked at Amelia, trying to lighten the mood.

Amelia's face lightened to sunburn pink, rendering her even more attractive and in charge. "He never married. No family mentioned in his file, so it's unclear how he got from spending time at an Amish colony in his youth to the list of foster homes listed. One brother MIA from the Gulf conflict. Parents died in a car accident. That's where it gets fuzzy between the Amish and the foster homes."

The shiver up and down my spine caught me by surprise. Samantha. Her beautiful heart-shaped face came into my mind, superimposed over faceless shapes in the foster system. I was praying before I realized it. *God, thank you for plucking her out of there and into my heart, into my home, into my life.*

"Yeah, well lots of *great* kids live in foster homes too." I stubbornly defended kids in the system every chance I got.

"The guy raises dogs and makes them fight each other for sport. I'm thinking that's not so good." Amelia had a hand on her hip.

"Yeah, sure. But killing dogs is different than killing people." *Not all that different, not really.* "But, you've definitely got to keep him in the mix."

"Not the one he wants us to believe," I said. "But, okay, I'll play along. What else do we know about good ol' Melvin White? Besides his cruelty to animals phase, how'd he wind up running a convenience store, and where's the guy from?"

"His geography works a little better for me." Amelia brightened. "He's got two convenience stores. One in Waupun and another in Portage."

"Puts him in between one set of murders and dead-on-the-money for the third." Nick smacked his hand on the table top.

"Slow down, Slick. I'm not buying it. Too convenient." I said. "Anything that looks that obvious … well, can't be." It wasn't very scientific, but it just didn't feel right to me. But I *was* right. I could *feel* it.

"Sometimes the obvious *is* the answer." Amelia was scanning files as she talked.

"And sometimes the obvious, or what's obvious to you, tends to shield you from what's right in front of you." I wasn't sure why I was so dead set against White being the killer, but I was. *Always trust your gut.*

"They know each other. They 'met' in my class. Burdock finds White. Killer instincts." Nick's voice had dropped back down to normal. He'd gone from almost over the edge to taking it all in. Amazing what a few facts could do for the psyche.

We sat around the table looking at each other without speaking for several seconds. I couldn't have been the only one wondering why the two chief suspects had decided to take an FBI class together. Or what they did for fun outside of class.

"So, they meet each other. That doesn't mean they kill together." I looked from Nick to Amelia and back as if I expected to see confirmation in their eyes. I didn't. I saw blank stares tinged with fear. *Did* they kill together? Were they planning to kill together again? I pointed at White's photo next to the victims. "It's entirely possible that he's the next target."

Amelia sighed. "Whether they're co-conspirators or hunter and prey almost doesn't matter. What does matter is we'll all be to blame if we don't figure out where the killer's going to strike next."

CHAPTER SEVENTEEN

I leaned back in my seat. "But I don't get it. Why would the killer show his hand by copying Nick's pattern theory? He'd have to know he'd be relatively easy to catch."

"Apparently not *that* easy—we're five bodies in." Nick's voice was flat with defeat. His fingers curled and uncurled around the armrests of his chair.

"Why is he painting the target on the bull's eye now? What's different?" It hit me as I formed the questions. "He's got an endpoint in mind." I paused. The two suits had already done the math, Nick too. "And?"

Amelia and Nick exchanged glances. She stepped away from the whiteboard and sat down, pushing the remote over to Nick. He brought up the kill map on the screen.

"So, if we apply the simple distance theory to what I'm referring to as the up side of the *Y*, how many towns fit that same mileage, that same radius?"

He'd finally spoken the question we'd no doubt all been asking ourselves. Nick studied the map, alternating between punching in numbers on his phone and circling names of towns in red that matched the relative distance coordinates from the down side of the *Y*. After he'd circled about a dozen names, he stepped back from the map, arms folded.

"So, this latest site, Reedsburg, it's an exact match to your pattern, isn't it?" I knew my hometown geography well enough. What I didn't know was how precise the killer might be. But then again, in investigations, everything stayed on the table until proven or disproven.

Nick nodded. "Why else would he choose Reedsburg? Why not North Freedom? Or Merrimac?" Nick tapped the remote pen on the table. "He had other choices. But he chose Reedsburg. That has to matter."

"Because that's where his victim presented?" I offered.

Dixon rose to her feet. "Fine. He chose Reedsburg. So, what's his next choice? What's the magic minute or mile spread?"

"If it *is* a spread. Let's assume it's dead-on. What towns lie within thirty-one minutes and a twenty-mile radius of Reedsburg, focusing on the north?" Nick looked from the map to me.

I stepped closer to the map, mulling over the possibilities. "My first guess is a little different than yours. I'd go with Wonewoc."

Nick shook his head.

"But it's circled." I sounded like a child.

"Yes, but it's not exact. It's only around twenty minutes, max." He shrugged. "It's possible. Just not my top choice."

My eyes followed the map a little farther north. "So, that leaves, what, Richland Center?"

"Maybe, but it feels too far off the beaten path to me." Nick squinted at the map.

"Viroqua then?"

"No, still too far to the west in my humble opinion."

I sighed. I hated guessing games. "Fine. What's left? Have you landed on Hillsboro?"

Hillsboro was a stop on the map between any number of small towns and of course the beautiful state park called Wildcat Mountain. It'd been one of my favorite places on earth when I was in high school. We'd "take a fade" from our classes for the day, jump in the car of whoever had the most gas money in their pocket and head for the hinterlands.

Making up plausible stories in case we got caught was my responsibility. We never got caught. After the statute of limitations had passed on getting mad at your kids for youthful indiscretions, I'd started to share parts of stories with my mom. She was not amused.

"Bull's-eye." Nick pressed a button on the remote, and a detailed map of Hillsboro popped up. Something budged in the far corner of my mind.

The corner of the screen featured a photo of a horse and buggy clip-clopping down the middle of a tree-lined street in the fall. The colors were otherworldly. Serene.

Hillsboro was right in the middle of Amish country. I'd attended summer festivals there when I was in high school. My girlfriends and I had taken it upon ourselves to befriend the local Amish teens, defending them against any kids looking to make fun of them for their counter-cultural upbringing. This earned us no end of points and latitude with the adults in our lives, thinking we were all about helping our neighbor at such a young age. We kept the real reason to our inner circle.

Those Amish guys were seriously hot. Clean-faced, muscular boys dressed in black danced through my head while I pulled up data on my phone. "Population 1,435. Village proper takes up less than two square miles." I looked up at Amelia and Nick, both still standing like big cats ready to pounce on not-yet-seen prey.

"Let's keep every single one of them alive, shall we?" Amelia's icy tone told me she was mentally prepping to get her teams on the road. "Tell me more."

Nick and I exchanged glances. We'd both shared a few takedowns with Amelia over the years. Some special agents loosened up in the field. Amelia buttoned down. Fine by me. A crackerjack agent, she could have my back anytime. I winked at Nick.

Nick squeezed my leg under the table as I tapped the remote on the surface.

"There's a significant Amish presence. All through that part of Wisconsin, up to and pretty much on all sides of Wildcat Mountain." I heard myself talking as if from a distance. It wasn't looking good for Melvin White.

Amelia tapped her lip. "Wait a minute, how far is Wildcat Mountain from Hillsboro?"

Nick sat down across the table from her and pulled out his laptop. "Hillsboro and Wildcat Mountain are practically on top of each other. The state park's a mile outside of town, tops."

"And White's store, right?" Hector reminded us of his recent find as he spun his laptop around to face us. "But look at this— we've made the front page." Staring at us was the homepage for Madison's WMTV.

The top of the website contained one bold headline: *Bowtie Killer Keeping the FBI in Knots.*

"Bowtie Killer?" Nick said.

"What the f … fridge?" Amelia said.

"Who's the leak?" I said.

Hector scrolled down the page, showing the length of the unauthorized article. "Don't shoot me. I'm just the messenger." He added. "No one's more surprised than me. We've been monitoring media sites for a while now, and I guarantee you this just came in."

"Awfully suspicious timing." Nick's growl wasn't directed at Hector. "Who the heck would tip the press? And why?"

"Did you say you sent pictures over? Get into the employee logs, and see who's working right now." Amelia directed her orders to Hector.

Hector stopped playing his keyboard. "Whoa. This is … interesting."

"And?" Amelia trained her eyes on him.

"Janice White is working right now. Hold on. I'm checking." Hector typed furiously.

"White? As in a relative of Melvin White?" It didn't seem possible, but the coincidence of the same name seemed less likely still.

"I thought you said he had no next of kin?" Nick was suspicious. I'd know that tone anywhere.

"Does a niece count?" Hector was a puppy. Grinning while setting his toy at the feet of his master. "Janice White. Daughter of Terrance White, Melvin's brother."

"The one that's allegedly MIA?" Amelia was on her feet, pacing.

"Must've been around long enough to sire a daughter." Maybe not one of my most helpful observations ever, but still.

Nick rolled his eyes at me. "So, who'd she call? And why?"

"More importantly, is she still there? Hector?" Amelia kept her attention on Hector.

At the sound of his name, Hector came alive at the keyboard once again. He jerked his head, stopped typing, and looked up. "No. She isn't. She signed out two hours ago."

"She meet him somewhere?" This was getting weirder and weirder. "And if so, what does that even mean? Is she in on this?" I could see the threads hanging before me, but I couldn't string them together.

"Why go to the press?" Hector's fingers were still flying. It was a good question.

"Because he knows we're on to him." Nick's voice grew deadly still. The kind of quiet where the bad guy pulls out a sword and looks the good guy in the eye from across a sandy camp.

"Because I asked the evidence tech about the gloves?" Something interesting was happening behind Hector's special-agent mask.

And suddenly, I saw it too. "Yup. You tripped his tip-up." I looked at Nick for confirmation.

He gave me a slight nod. He didn't usually appreciate my use of ice-fishing imagery.

"Holy crap," I said. "This guy is a lot smarter than your average bear."

"And he doesn't hunt alone," Nick added.

The suspects grinned from the screen. Alex Burdock, thirty-five-year-old, garden-variety single American male. Loner by night, bowtie-wearing do-gooder by day. What happened when the bowtie came off?

Melvin White, corn-fed country boy with a temper and animal-abuse history, keeping the home fires burning in a couple of convenience stores. Ties to the Amish community, Hillsboro, and Wildcat Mountain. I saw a blue line leading from Madison to all three places in my mind's GPS.

"Where do they find their victims? Are they hunting them?" What I was really wondering was how many more Nick lookalikes could they find?

Amelia's look could wither steel. "We've *got* to find more real commonalities between these two, find solid evidence linking them to the murder vics."

"Right. But we don't exactly have a plethora of information to chew through on that front." I stared up at White and Burdock. "Of all the classes in the world, Burdock shows up in yours, sitting next to a guy who looks like you."

"Can you think of anything either of them said during class discussion?" Amelia rested her chin on one hand, propping it up with the other and paced.

Wrong turn. "Forget the trip down memory lane. Where did they meet the vics?" I raised my eyes to the ceiling, picturing sun-drenched ads luring people to Wisconsin, targeted at residents of neighboring states. "Festivals? Jamborees? Summer camping?"

Nick tented his fingers and rested his head on the tips. "It *is* the land of milk and honey. Wouldn't be the first friendship forged over a campfire between strangers."

Nick dropped his hands to the table. "Wait a minute. Fishing! What if they're connected by fishing? Josie, didn't you say something about tip-ups a few minutes ago?"

"Yeah, but—"

"The first vic, staged to look like an ice-fishing accident, right?" Nick's face was flushed, his fingers forming a map of Wisconsin on the wood table, pointing to Crandon by tapping his finger on the glossy wood surface. "What if they met their first vic fishing?"

"Be a heckuva clue, killing him like that." I bit my thumbnail. "Course, maybe it happened spontaneously. Maybe it wasn't planned."

Nick drummed his fingers on the wood table. "Isn't there some sort of ice fishing and snowmobiling extravaganza in Northern Wisconsin every winter? Maybe that's where they met victim number one."

Amelia had been feverishly jotting down notes during our conversation. She stood still, pen and notebook in hand, gazing above our heads at the screen. "We're getting close on both sides of the equation. Nick, Josie, do some digging on the ice-fishing angle." Nick and I snapped open our computers and fired them up.

Amelia raised an eyebrow and looked at Hector. "They'd have to stay somewhere, right? Comb through every hotel, motel, mom-and-pop stand and campground between Portage and Crandon."

Hector let out a big breath and turned to the agent next to him. "Start with the state tourism websites."

I popped my head up. "Google might be faster."

Hector rolled his eyes. "We know what we're doing."

Amelia unfolded her arms, pinching the skin between her eyebrows. "Hector, text Agents Roscoe and Landry. See if they've got anything of interest from their search and rescue mission on the dating sites. And put another on the data surf for the Escape to Wisconsin snowmobiling, ice fishing, and camping connection. This has got to break wide open. Soon."

Hector stretched his neck, followed by his palms. He ended his stretch break by bending one finger at a time over the edge of the table. Renewed, his hands flew once again across the keyboard, stopping with a definitive punch on the Enter button when he'd finished. He looked up at Amelia Dixon, hands hovering over his keyboard. "What now, boss?"

"Now we get ready to Escape to Wisconsin. Saddle up, boys." I interrupted, mind filled with gruesome pictures of Kyle Wirth spread across the Welcome to Reedsburg sign. "We're going."

Amelia stiffened, pushing away from the table. "Isn't that my decision to make?" She leveled gray-green eyes at me.

"Sure. That's why I asked. We're going?" I raised my palms up, giving what I hoped was an innocent tilt of my head.

"Uh-huh." Her deadpan tone told me she wasn't buying it. "It's the right place for us to lay in wait for the creep. We're back on Nick's original idea." She nodded at him.

Amelia held her hand up, her eyes glued to her computer screen. "Stop everything. Landry found it. Geoffrey Spencer, the first vic, from Crandon, registered for the 2016 New Year's Day Fisheree and Polar Bear Swim, in Crandon, stayed two nights at a Holiday Inn on the outskirts of town. As did one M. White and an Alex Burdock. And they shared a room." Amelia looked up at us. "I'd say our case just went all the way live."

CHAPTER EIGHTEEN

"Hector, get four agents on the road, two to canvass Spencer's neighbors one more time. Have them ask about New Year's weekend in particular. Did the vic talk about it? Bring home friends? See what pops."

"On it." Hector stood to attention.

"Get the other two on the road to that Holiday Inn. Have them push the same angles and anything else that moves." Amelia nodded at Hector, and he was the out the door.

Amelia turned her laser gaze to us. "Should I be comfortable with your best guess for his next step?"

"Given that Reedsburg and Portage are equidistant from Baraboo, Hillsboro really does make perfect sense. On paper." I rubbed my chin. "It seems like such a neat package. Could these guys really be imitating Nick's classroom example so precisely? And if so, why be so obvious? What're they trying to tell us?" My temples started to throb.

Nick and Amelia exchanged a look that went uncomfortably long. *Uh-oh.*

"What? What's going on? What are you two afraid of?" I looked from one to the other.

Neither spoke for several seconds. Nick stretched his neck and blinked. "It all points to the same thing. An ending of sorts. A finale. A last hurrah."

Amelia nodded.

"You don't get this intentional and start handing out these loud clues without a reason."

"Yeah, I'm getting that. But what's the reason? Telling us we're stupid? Or they're tired of working for a living and wants their three squares on Uncle Sam's dime? Or that they're tired of working *and* of living?" Suicide by cop was not uncommon with violent criminals. But, this all seemed awfully elaborate for such a tired ending.

"Burdock's definitely triggered by Nick, wants to draw him in, show him up. He might've got impatient. Pointing the thunderbird's wingtip to Josie's lot was a smart way to seal the Nick deal." Amelia addressed the wall over our heads, trancelike, arms folded again. "But why? Did the suspects meet in class, or did they wind up in his class because they learned about the switch to Nick after Max died?"

I'd wondered the same thing, just not out loud. Mostly because I didn't like any of the conceivable answers. No matter which thread might start being unraveled by any of the possible answers, they all ultimately led to a showdown in Hillsboro. And if we were about to go off in the wrong direction altogether—then our troubles were just beginning.

"So, we head to Hillsboro. What's our cover? What've they got up there besides Amish farmers and cheddar cheese?" Nick seemed anxious.

Winter, spring, summer, or fall. There wasn't a bad season for Wildcat Mountain as far as I was concerned. I could drive it in my sleep. And more often than not, back in the day, we'd stop in Hillsboro coming or going. Sometimes for pop, BBQ Corn Nuts, and M&M's, and sometimes just for a potty break. Once, we'd broken our pattern and stopped on a weekday, early evening. And got quite a treat. "They still doing those auctions?"

Nick and Amelia stared at me, and then at each other.

Hector looked up at that in time to answer my question with one of his own. He directed it to Amelia. "You got my text? About the auctions?"

Amelia nodded. "Agents recovered visits to the Hillsboro Amish Auction House website from Burdock's online search history. We've got him."

"Booyah!" Hector threw a fist in the air.

"What do you know about that auction house, Jo? Why is he going there?"

"Auctions are chaotic. Could make an ideal spot for a grab. I know they used to have live horse auctions. Probably still do, nothing much changes fast in small towns."

The fledgling thought had sprouted wings and flown into my past. And an unplanned stop had segued into an adventure for me. "I met a cowboy at a gas station when I was in high school. I helped him prep horses for the sale ring. Best first date ever. Antiques, odds and ends, and lots of other stuff hit the block from noon to four p.m. I remember we had a few hours to get the horses ready before the auction started right back up at six p.m. sharp."

I could see myself as a teenage girl, clad in tight blue jeans, my best pair of boots, cinching up the horses, giving them one last rub down before throwing a leg up, riding them into the tiny sales ring, loudspeaker blaring.

Amelia looked at her phone. "So, that gives us a little over six hours before the auction starts. Means Burdock's probably in the area or headed there from wherever he hides out." Amelia leaned forward, lips pursed. "I'm sending in advance teams now to cover the auction house. Two inside—"

"No offense, Amelia, but your guys will stick out like donkeys at a horse show. You'd be better off sending me up there. Time's a wasting, and if there's one thing I know, it's horses. And my way around an auction barn."

Nick gave me an appreciative glance. "All the distractions of prepping for an evening auction should make it that much easier for us to blend in, wait him out."

Amelia nodded for Hector to get up, all the while typing out orders into her iPhone.

Hector stood up, shutting his laptop down, awaiting his master's orders.

"Much as I'd love to keep you here at the computer, Hector, I'll send you with the chief to the scene in Hillsboro." Hector looked at her, unable to keep the smile dancing in his eyes from spreading to his lips.

"Trust me. You don't want this one, Hector." I started to object but thought better of it. Sending Nick with me would tip the killer off. Besides, while I knew how to blend in, there was no way to hide his Italian sophistication in the middle of all of those flannel shirts and open twelve-packs of Budweiser and Pabst Blue Ribbon. I sighed and turned to Hector. "Lucky you. This is undercover work of the nastiest sort. It's definitely not for everyone. Ever ridden a horse before?" I looked over at Nick and winked.

He stood next to me, rolling his foot against mine under the table. "Stay close to Chief Oliver. These are her people. She'll know what to do. And for Pete's sake, try not to say anything. Those hicks will suss you out faster 'n a summer strike of lightning."

Nick nudged my heel with his so suddenly I almost lost my balance. Heat rose up my neck, flushing my face. I'd broken in any number of detectives over my years on the force, and more than one had since graduated to a successful career as a special agent. But only one had ever come close to breaking me. And he wouldn't be riding shotgun with me this time.

CHAPTER NINETEEN

Agent Dixon finished the briefing and sent us all off in different directions. Hector and I would serve as an undercover advance team, scouting the area and reporting back from the road as quickly as possible. Amelia would coordinate all field efforts with other agencies while staying behind at headquarters, and Nick headed out to gather the troops as head of ground operations. Literally. Scores of well-trained men and women would soon be at our disposal as we made our way toward the Hillsboro area in what I was told would be a rusted-out Ford pickup of questionable condition. *We should blend right in.*

"What should I expect from 'your people'?" Hector grinned at me as we headed to the elevators together. "And what am I wearing to this redneck affair?"

I looked him up and down, eyebrow raised. "Definitely not that." The elevator opened. "How about a long-sleeved flannel shirt, off-brand jeans with a belt, and scuffed boots? And a seasoned baseball cap. Wardrobe gonna have anything close to that?"

Hector stepped up to the panel and pressed the button labeled *B*. "We'll see."

When the elevator door opened again, we'd been transported to a behind-the-scenes madhouse. Chain-link fence separated us from a wide open, windowless floor plan that must've run the length of the building. Florescent lights lent an artificial glow to a series of exposed rabbit dens containing unexpected vignettes.

Agents and artists were grouped together as precisely as if seated in cookie-cutter cubicles. Most groupings contained what looked like one grumpy special agent being attended to by two flamboyant professionals wielding the tools of their trade—attempting to deliver faux tattoos, kicky new hairdos, and all manner of creative makeup enhancements.

Hector nudged me. "You about ready to move on?"

A navy-clad female agent had unlocked a door to the cage in front of us and stood waiting to usher us in. She had blunt-cut chestnut hair and might as well have been rolling her eyes at us.

"Oh, I'm sorry. Are we keeping you from your appointment?" I leaned toward her, close enough to read her nametag. "Special Agent Lowry?"

She snorted and shook her head. "Nope. I've got all the time in the world to wait for a hometown hero."

Her voice was a swath of light rolling back clouds in my mind, revealing a 1970 cherry-red Mach I Ford. She and I drinking sparkling cider, solving all our sixteen-year-old problems, sitting on its hood under a perfect summer sky, stars and moon colliding with our laughter.

"Amy? So, you really are a brunette?" She'd been a blonde in high school.

She snorted again. "That's all you got, Oliver? I haven't seen you in twenty years, and that's the best you can do?" Amy stepped into my personal space, hands resting on hips.

"You gonna hug me or deck me?" I grinned at her, wandering through memories that included stealing each other's booze and the occasional boyfriend. I searched her eyes, wondering which kind of memory would surface last.

"Aw, hell. I ain't into massacres. C'mere." She moved in, bringing both arms around me in a tight hug. Her arms were massive.

I returned the hug, quickly pulling back and putting space between us. "How long have you been here?" It was awkward. But it beat going down any number of personal paths I couldn't be sure about. I'd heard that the years and life, in general, had been unkind to her. But then, she'd probably heard the same thing about me. "And where are you living these days?"

"Ten years and none of your business." She crossed her arms and stepped back against the fencing, one foot propped up, nodding her head down the hall just beyond her.

I raised my eyebrows and gave her my winningest smile as we walked past her. I had a pretty good idea of which remnant of our shared histories was sticking her in the ribs right now, but I wasn't sure I was as responsible for the fallout as she remembered. Sure, I may have been a tad indiscreet in my youth. *Ease up on me.* I was only sixteen.

Hector walked a few steps ahead of me all the way to the wardrobe closet lining the back wall of the pen. "You and GI Jane seemed none too friendly. What'd you do to her?"

I snorted. "We don't have that much time. Show me what you got in here instead."

My phone rang as I opened a door labeled with white stenciling. *Wardrobe Locker.* I checked the phone and hit Answer, smiling. "To what do I owe the pleasure?"

"*Mija*, there is always pain before the pleasure with you. Perhaps you will allow me to minimize the pain with an interesting little device that will round out your hunting gear." Gino Rivera's voice filled my ear.

I stood in the locker room, exhaling a long breath. His voice was as potent as fresh-cut lavender. I closed my eyes and basked in the soothing image of Gino, my drop-dead gorgeous Cuban partner in crime and spiritual guide.

I'd met Gino six months before Nick tornadoed into my world. It was Gino who'd helped me sort out my feelings for Nick, Gino who'd been there for me when I was in desperate need of salvation in every sense of the word. Solid as a big brother, better than dark chocolate, Gino was just what the doctor ordered. *Too bad I ignored his pleadings not to marry Del.*

"What've you got?" I asked. I knew he'd have been fully briefed before calling. Fast work, even for Nick.

"You are searching for a killer who seems to be baiting you, no?"

"Yes." I drew the word out long and slow, wondering what he could be up to.

"And a killer who taunts you is a killer who is escalating, *verdad?*"

"Yes." *What do you have up your sleeve?* In addition to being one of my dearest friends in life, Gino was also a world-renowned designer of search, pursuit, capture, and restraint technologies. You'd never know it from his humble spirit.

"So, he is a man begging to be lured, to be chased, to be captured. And I have just the thing for you." Gino was a man of his word, and he knew his way around the criminal element. Given the confidence in his voice, I was dying to see what he had in mind.

"I'm sold, G. When can we meet up?"

Hector was staring at me, listening. I gave him the once-over, walked over to a rack of jeans and tossed a tattered pair at him.

"As soon as you finish Hector's makeover." His deep voice chuckled into my ear, and then he was gone.

I shook my head. Hector had disappeared into a changing room. My phone vibrated as a text came in from Gino. "Meet me in Reedsburg on your way to Hillsboro."

If it had been anybody but Gino, I'd be surprised. Maybe even a little creeped out. But Gino had enough connections to keep him in the know on everything from when the McRib was coming back on the market to the latest intel on pretty much all local investigations. He was a former Navy Seal and had more than one "brother" here in Madison's FBI field office.

Hector emerged, looking less like a federal agent and more like a rodeo wannabe. Still not a hundred percent local but better than he'd been in the dead-giveaway monkey suit. I sighed. He probably wouldn't blend in all that well at the Amish auction house, but it'd have to do.

"Let's go." I headed out of the cage.

"That was Gino Rivera, I presume?" Hector walked a step behind me as we made our way back to the elevator.

Special Agent Amy Lowry gave me the stink eye when we passed by her. She hadn't moved an inch and was probably watching us the whole time we shopped the wardrobe. I stepped into the elevator, smiling and waving at her as the doors slid shut.

"I don't think she liked you, Hector."

"Yeah. It was all about me, Chief. Alright if I call you Chief?" His voice cracked.

"Fine by me." I studied my phone, nodding at the guards as we made our way out of the building. The rumbling in my stomach suggested we should meet Gino at The Pleased Pig. By the time I finished texting this fact to Gino, Hector was standing by the passenger door of our new chariot. It was exactly what we'd asked for—a rusted-out Ford pickup, cream-colored with red pinstripes that may have been popular a few decades ago.

"Looks like something you and your friend Ms. Lowry would be comfortable driving." Hector grinned at me as he slid across the bench seat and buckled up.

I rolled my eyes at him, hoping to shut him down. Talking about my colorful past was not on the agenda. Besides, I liked him a lot better when he kept his mouth shut.

"We're heading to a dive called The Pleased Pig in Reedsburg. That's where we'll meet up with Gino and get our cover stories straight." I started the truck. It sounded tired.

"I can't believe I'm finally going to get a chance to meet and actually work with the legendary Gino Rivera. Amelia approved him carte blanche. Means he can do whatever it takes to assist in the investigation. I guess he defines 'whatever it takes.'"

I smiled at his boyish enthusiasm. "Yup. He's earned it."

He nodded. "Rank does have its privileges."

"With any luck at all, we'll catch these guys, and you'll have something to take back to headquarters for show-and-tell." I steered out of the parking garage into the streets.

We were navigating through Madison on our way to the belt line before he spoke again. "So, you're wearing what you've got on?"

I frowned at him and glanced quickly down at the boot-cut jeans, well-worn black Ariats, and the Green Bay Packers' vest I'd snatched from the FBI's wardrobe locker to cover my favorite blue velour hoodie. I reached behind the seat, rummaging around until I found the dusty black cowboy hat I'd been promised, freshly delivered from the Bureau's basement, and put it on. It was all Wisconsin, all the time. I gave myself a rapid once-over, right palm up and slicing through the air with authority. "Yup. Dressed for success."

"Are you taking CO for this part of the mission?" His use of police jargon was intentional. No doubt he didn't like the idea of me being his commanding officer for the junket.

"Yup." I emphasized the *P* with a loud pop.

"Then, you look mahvalous, Chief."

I raised an eyebrow in his direction. "I didn't know they'd added a sense of humor to your make and model."

"Country upgrade. Goes with these fine DeeCee jeans, don't you think?" So, Hector was carrying a slight grudge over my clothing choices for him. *Good. Give him a little humility maybe.*

"Sure thing. Should be enough to drive the country girls and Amish maidens absolutely wild when they see you strutting your stuff in a few." I pictured him attempting to charm the clientele we were about to encounter and very nearly laughed out loud.

His olive skin turned autumnal red. I ground my hands into the steering wheel, stifling my enjoyment. "Something's missing ... Oh, I know. Don't worry, gotcha covered." I pulled over to the curb and put the truck in park, rummaging through the glove box until I found what no self-respecting truck owner would be without. "Heads up."

Hector flinched, catching the little round tin midair. "Redman?"

I laughed out loud, watching him turn the palest of light browns. "Looks like this *is* your first rodeo, amigo."

CHAPTER TWENTY

It was just after one p.m. when we pulled into an angled parking space in front of The Pleased Pig, one of Gino's favorite spots for reconnoitering.

"So, this is where we meet your infamous Captain Amazing?" Hector unbuckled his seat belt.

I searched the street for Gino's Z28. "Yup. Don't see his car anywhere though. I'm pretty sure he has no reason to fly under the radar."

"Wake me up when it's over." Hector sighed and crossed his arms.

"No problem. In the meantime, you mind if I play cop and keep my eyes peeled for a serial killer?" I didn't hide my annoyance.

He stiffened. "You really think Bowtie Guy is lurking somewhere around here?"

"You can't think of one reason why our killer would be in Reedsburg." *Idiot.* What did they teach these guys in special agent school anyway? "Anything come to mind? Like a dead body draped over the Welcome to Reedsburg sign?"

"Fine." He put his seat back and stretched out his legs. "How solid do you really believe the theory about this Hicksboro town is, anyway?"

"You know, if I talked like that about where you grew up, you'd probably slap a discrimination suit on me." I stretched my fingers one by one.

"Probably. You were saying? About Hillsboro?"

"Rock solid. That's not what worries me." I reviewed the killer's map in my mind. "The vics. Where's he find these guys? How does he know where to hunt?"

Hector drummed his fingers lightly on the passenger door handle. "Where would you find five men of the same make and model, to quote you."

"Where indeed. Unless …" A theory was materializing and pushing past the fog in my brain.

"What are you thinking?" He stopped drumming and looked over at me.

"It's a long shot, I think. But that lineup. It reminded me of a dating website. What if the meet-ups were online?"

"It makes sense. It'd have to be a visual medium. Killer had to have access to fairly recent pix. Why not a dating website?" He pulled out his phone and texted someone.

"Just like that, you've got another set of agents running this down? And you're getting around privacy laws?"

He nodded.

"But you're not illegally hacking?"

He shrugged.

I whistled. "Where'd you guys perfect your ability to blur the lines like that?"

"Spy school." He didn't elaborate. But he did crane his neck as Gino's black Z28 rumbled into the parking spot next to us.

I jumped out of the truck. My smile spread involuntarily. Quality time with Gino Rivera always made me happy.

Gino welcomed me into his arms, infusing me with warmth. The light that seemed to follow him lifted me from the inside. A sudden assurance that everything would be alright saturated my body at the cellular level. I pulled away from him, threw my shoulders back and took the arm he offered.

We were headed into the restaurant when Gino jabbed his head in Hector's direction. "Your Agent Newbie?"

"Yup." I didn't break my stride.

"Fed. With a solid track record." It wasn't a question.

"Yup." I ducked under his arm and into The Pleased Pig. For a vegetarian joint, it sure smelled a lot like bacon.

Gino held the door for Hector, and we settled into one of four booths. Five or six Formica tables rounded out the seating selection. I knew from experience we'd chosen the more comfortable option.

A tall Amish man dressed in a long black duster walked in front of the diner's window. A tall hat pulled low rendered his features indistinguishable. He glanced in, and for a moment he stared right at me. *I've seen those eyes before.* A wave of dizziness rolled over me, and images of tortured people in dark places zipped through my mind. Involuntary shivers raced up my body, and I shut my eyes, gave my head a slight shake and shrugged my shoulders up and down in an effort to find a reset from my fright. *I've got to get more sleep.*

Gino turned around, following my eyes. "Jo?"

I looked up at the window, my heart dropping into my boots. The man was gone. Between Gino using my real name and the dread shooting straight through me from the stranger's eyes, something bad was in the air. *Really bad.* I breathed in deeply, centering myself, willing away the sense of foreboding that still clung to the edges of my mind. *Shake it off, Oliver.*

I looked over at my wise friend. "Your supernatural senses tingling again?"

"Sí, *mija.* You could call it hyperdrive. Let's order our meal to go."

"Just in case," I said to Hector, who shook his head.

"The guys aren't going to believe me when I tell them how you roll."

For the trip to Hillsboro, I surrendered the truck to Hector and rode shotgun with Gino. He drove the sports car with masterful precision, sliding around hairpin turns awash in the lime, chartreuse, and hunter greens of Wisconsin in all her springtime glory. I opened the passenger window, inhaling the luxuriously crisp air, bringing hints of rich soil and new possibilities into the car with us as we ate vegan burritos from paper wrappers. Gino was smiling. Tension siphoned off my shoulders, leaving me feeling much lighter.

Gino's smile retreated a notch as I bagged our trash and tucked it down by my feet. "Shall we now speak of whatever is going on between you and the ever-delightful Saint Nicolas?"

I let go of a noisy breath, tossing in an eye roll any teen would envy, in case he missed my message. "If you insist."

"*Mija*, you both have the iron souls only the Master himself can create." Gino was going to speak mystic today. *Great.*

"I'm not really in the mood for your puzzle talk, G."

"Says the woman of a thousand faces. All worn to protect her heart." He pursed his lips, speeding up to meet the base of a new curve. "Let me put it to you like this. You have a good man on the run. For what? To punish him even more than he has already punished himself?"

His words stunned me. I wasn't punishing anyone. Least of all Nick. "How can you even say that?" Prickling heat crawled up the base of my neck. "And, I might have an update—"

"You push him away from you in the hospital after he put his heart on the line for you. And that after he nearly got disciplined for over-involving you in his last case." His voice had taken on a steely tone I didn't like and wasn't used to.

I was desperate to tell him we were back together. Sort of. *I think.* I leaned forward to speak, and he held up a finger. "No, you can listen for a split second longer. Think of it from his point of view. Think like a proud man. He lays himself out for you, you reject him, and you turn him away." Gino's eyes were shiny. He gripped the wheel tighter. "And he obeys you. He leaves your room. And ..." The veins in his hands bulged.

I knew what he was thinking, why he couldn't speak. I closed my eyes tight, pushing away the vision of Kira leaning over me with a hypodermic needle loaded for bear. Kira Stoklavich had nearly ended my life moments after Nick had left my room. I placed my hand on Gino's.

Gino looked at me, one tear rolling silently down his rugged cheek. My eyes started stinging, and my throat tightened. "But I'm okay, G. I'm okay." I clasped his hand tight against my chest.

"Yet, you cannot imagine how almost losing you, moments after he left you defenseless in a hospital room, has affected him. Nick, our Nick, is not as strong as you think, *mija*. He bleeds. He pines. He yearns for you."

"I know he does. I do. I just don't know if I can trust it to last." I let go of his hand and placed a hand on my chest. Hot flames flushed my face as I thought of the one word that came to mind first whenever I thought of Nick these days: *trust*. Would I ever be able to fully trust a man again?

Gino accelerated into another curve, easily navigating the steep country road. I glanced into my side mirror. "Hector must've received an *A* in defensive driving school."

Gino's hand shot to the rearview mirror. "Excellent. He drives like a Latino."

"What's that supposed to mean?"

"He's fearless. Watch that one. I looked into him. He'll go far. Heart of a lion." Gino glanced at the rearview mirror again and smiled approvingly.

Of course Gino had checked him out. "Yup. Big dog in a little dog's body." I sat up and pulled my cell phone out of my purse. I stabbed Hector's number into my phone. "We haven't exactly planned our next move." How had I been so careless?

Hector talked around a mouthful of his own lunch. "How many moves can there be? We go to Hillsboro. We find the man, and we bring him in. That is your plan."

Gino stretched his neck and nodded to a sign on my side of the road. Hillsboro. Eleven miles.

My back muscles tightened. "Crap. Here's what we do, Jaime."

"Jaime? The best you can do is Jaime?" Hector's voice must've reached Gino.

A wry smile spread across his face as he drove.

"Yup. Jaime. We're horse trainers from a track in Illinois, and you're looking for a race buggy." Gino's eyebrows popped up as I spoke. "And I'm your assistant."

"My bossy, annoying assistant, named Brunhilda." If Hector was nervous, I couldn't tell from his voice.

"Let's stick to Brenda. Brenda Hill. We're both from the Arlington Heights area, near the track. Gino's pulling over, and I'll jump into the truck so we can hit the auction barn together." I glanced over at Gino, smiling as he slowed down and pulled the car over. "The place will be full on auction day, so we go in soft. Amelia's got local cops and agents heading there too."

"Wish me luck, amigo." I kissed Gino on the cheek and slid out of the car.

"My prayers and my heart are always with you, *mija*. Though this time, I'll be there too. In the shadows." He winked as I closed the door and nodded at him.

"What are you waiting for?" I buckled my seatbelt and stared at Hector impatiently. "He's waiting for us to pull out." Adrenaline coursed through me. "This ain't *my* first rodeo, Jaime. So, jump out in front and don't spare the horses."

Hector shook his head and drove the last few miles while hopefully soaking in all the useful cover details I spouted about horses, hicks, and life at the track. Hillsboro sprang up before us. A row of buildings that had seen better days ushered us to a stop sign.

"Main Street. Man, I love small town America. Which way, Chief?" The edge in Hector's voice generated waves of energy.

I took a deep breath, driving my thoughts back to high school and summer days full of horses and flirting with cute cowboys. "Turn left, go on down the road a good six or seven blocks and pull up into an angled parking spot on the right hand side of the road. The auction house will be on the other side of the street." Sudden assurance floated over me, and I knew beyond a shadow of a doubt that we were in the right place, at the right time. Burdock was here. I could feel it.

CHAPTER TWENTY-ONE

Hector eased the car into the last empty parking spot, turned the engine off and looked at me.

I didn't want to make it more complicated than it needed to be. "Leave the keys under the visor, up top."

His staring took on an alarmed quality.

I rolled my eyes at him. "It'll be fine. Hick Code of Honor. Trust me." I opened my door and got out with as much country cool as I could muster, channeling my inner cowgirl. My hips loosened up, and a long-forgotten swagger reasserted itself. *I still got it.*

I waited for Hector to catch up to me, and we crossed the street in unison, heads down, sporting the grim expressions of working race trainers. Hector looked genuinely nervous. I was pretty sure he wasn't acting.

The auction was housed in a round barn. It was rumored to be over a hundred fifty years old and had allegedly been "renovated" a few years back. From the looks of it, I was betting it had been an inside job, and that no Amish influence had been sought.

Hector's energy seemed to dissipate as we neared the barn door. "Just remember your ABCs, baby, and you'll be fine." I patted his elbow, turned the latch and pushed open the old wooden door.

We stepped into a darkness filled with layered noise. The ever-present drone of the auctioneer's voice fell around us as we walked toward the sale pen. By the time I'd planted myself across the board fence, one foot cocked behind me, the insistent mechanical voice had faded into background noise.

Hector stood to my left, watching the horses parading past us in the tiny arena. His arms were folded across his chest, and he'd found a long piece of hay to chew on. He looked for all the world like the real deal. *If they could see you now from their office suites in Manhattan.* I felt like a proud teacher sitting next to her eighth-grade spelling bee champ.

The staccato voice of the auctioneer ratcheted up several notches, and the crowd took on an electric air. In the sales pen, a dainty sorrel filly captured my attention. She had a teacup nose, a star and a blaze, and a set of hindquarters on her that could stop a freight train. She stood at only 14.2 hands, but she was flashy, and she could turn on a dime.

The number on her rump was fifty-two, and I paged through the catalog to learn more about her. Hector elbowed me, and I turned to him, nerves fraying. He tilted his hat to the right of the pen. The flashy young mare was turning and cantering off, spurred by a large man who looked like he might outweigh her. I shook my head and pulled my eyes off the beautiful little filly.

Movement on the outside of the pen caught my eye. A tall Amish man, hat pulled low over fair hair, was walking briskly away from the pen. My breath snagged in my throat, and my scalp tingled. He was the man I'd seen outside The Pleased Pig. Everything fell into place. Burdock. I hadn't been looking for him in costume.

"Stay here and act natural. Maybe throw in a bid on that mare. And text Amelia. Tell her I think we've found our man." I whispered orders out of the side of my mouth and left Hector standing by the pen.

Then, I took off at a fast walk in the direction of dusty, black, coat tails.

I followed the dark shape of the tall man away from the crowd. He glanced over his shoulder, but I didn't see his face—too busy being spooked by his eyes. It was Burdock, no doubt about it. Spotting me, he threw his head up and broke into a smooth jog, running down a row of pens full of restless animals. *Only the guilty flee for no reason, right?*

I pushed into a run and followed him around the pens, keeping one eye open for White—co-conspirator or victim, no one could say at this point. The round structure opened up into a large pole barn. Dust filled the air. Metal gears sprang to life fifty feet ahead of me. Someone was releasing feed from the corn crib down through the chute into a trough.

There was no sign of my Amish prey. I slowed to a walk. The round barn continued to my left, and the feed bin clanked on ahead of me somewhere beyond the yawning darkness of the pole barn. Animals shifted and banged the boards in their stalls, and horses nickered as I strode past them. The pole barn was filled with small pens on all four sides. A practice arena was set up in the middle, sandwiched by long wooden water troughs.

I walked through the sand of the arena, uncertain of my next move. *Lord, I need you now. Be with me. Guide me. Protect me ... Stop him.*

A deep sense of peace poured through me, invoking feelings of sitting in front of a warm hearth. Ammonia from soiled bedding wafted into the arena. I dug my feet into the sand, surrounded by stillness. A boot heel scraped against concrete near the back door.

I snapped my head in the direction of the noise and started running. The footsteps on concrete broke into a run. I hit the edge of the arena and lost my footing, nearly tumbling onto the cement floor. Light seeped under the bottom of the pole barn, drawing shadows across the darkened aisle. I stopped, breathing hard, realizing I hadn't heard his footsteps for the past several seconds.

An overwhelming, coppery odor filled my nostrils.

A sudden whoosh of air. Blinding pain. Darkness.

"Woman down!" A slender shadow knelt over me. Electronic static brought unintelligible sounds.

"Chief Oliver! Are you alright?" Hector's voice cut away the cobwebs wrapped around my brain.

I sat up. *Mistake.* Nausea rolled over me. I turned away from him and vomited. Fiery explosions rocketed through my head. "I'm fine."

I turned over onto my hands and knees, breathing deeply for several long seconds. The coppery smell of blood was thick. Hector's hand was on my shoulder. I pitched back onto my heels, grabbed his arm, and pulled myself shakily to my feet. "I'm fine."

I closed my eyes, straightening my clothes. When I opened them again, Gino stood before me, appraising me shrewdly. A circle of uniformed cops knelt over a figure in the sand.

"He's gone. We've got another vic. I called Amelia with an update, and we're in pursuit." He offered me an arm, and I took it.

Hot tears welled up as we passed the jeans-clad body of a dark-haired man in his forties. An auction house sticker with the letter *I* had been slapped onto the dead man's cheek. Waves of nausea flooded my stomach, and I let myself be carried away by my colleagues.

"I'm so sorry." I was shaking, my body trying to reset my mind.

We race-walked out of the barn into the blinding sunlight. Sandwiched between Hector and Gino, I stopped abruptly. Gino's Z28 was parked in an angled spot across the street from the spot where I was certain we'd left our truck less than thirty minutes earlier. I turned to Gino, confused. "The perp stole our truck?"

Hector scrambled into the back seat of Gino's car. It roared to life, and I buckled myself into the passenger seat. Gino maneuvered with measured speed around country corners, talking over his Bluetooth to an omnipresent crew of highly trained security personnel. He was barking coordinates and predictions of where the killer was headed like the former operative he was.

He mentioned Wildcat Mountain several times. My eyebrows shot up. How had he known? The rumble of a chopper overhead answered my question.

I shook my head, shooting Gino an appreciative glance. "Really, G?"

"Any man who puts my Josie on the ground has earned an all-star chase." Gino's features hardened into an unreadable mask as he reached out and squeezed my knee. The cell phone pinged again, and he pulled his hand away, gesticulating wildly as if winding himself up to respond.

Right before Gino's next cell phone tirade, the choked sound of repressed laughter caught my attention. I turned around slowly, wary of nausea and my wrenched neck and glared at my new partner. Hector froze, mid-shoulder-shaking laugh.

"Don't," I said, as menacingly as I could muster.

But he ignored my warning. "Hick Code of Honor, my—"

"Shut up." I turned around, gripping the passenger door handle as another tight curve rose before us.

Hector leaned forward from the back, gripping my seat. "So, we zoom after Burdock, but does he know all roads in

Hickdom belong to you? That Wildcat Mountain was named after you?"

Gino was still barking orders to his men as he navigated hairpin turns at dizzying speeds, switching from English to Spanish as easily as switching hands on the wheel.

I turned my head back to Hector. "Guy like that, he'd have spent plenty of time casing the roads, maybe the whole state."

My napkin-map of Wisconsin, with its crudely marked kill spots, came to mind. Burdock knew where he was going. Had to. But had he planned it like this? Or had we spooked him into running? I pictured the stream of letters in my mind. *J-E-ME-H-A-I* ... Nothing spelled any destination I could conceive of. Nothing made sense. But still, there was something familiar about this combination of letters.

The car phone erupted into a frenzied roar. Field agents reported into Amelia from a dozen different locations, shouting into phones and radios. Gino's system somehow relayed them all.

"He's fishtailing!"

"He's flipped!"

"Look at that!"

"Is he dead?"

"Whoa! He's running!"

"We've got a runner!"

Beads of sweat popped out above Gino's brow. "Where's he going? Is he injured?" His gravelly voice filled the interior. He punched the accelerator, and we rocketed around another curve, nearly at the top of the steep road.

I'd pulled a truck and trailer loaded with horses up this hill many times. Jackrabbited up it on my old Harley too. The mouth of Wildcat Mountain State Park and its complex series of heavily wooded trails was the pot of gold at the end of this rainbow. Was that where Burdock was headed?

"What have we here?" Gino's calm voice jarred me from my thoughts.

Several police cars were parked in the middle and on the side of the road. The cream-and-rust-colored Ford pickup lay upended in the ditch on the right. The driver's door was open—the cab empty. A clear set of fresh prints in the mud told the story. Burdock had gone to ground.

The entire jagged map of Wildcat Mountain drew itself in velvety colors in my mind's eye. Miles of trails crisscrossed under an endless canopy of pine, birch, walnut, and linden trees. The park was bordered on three sides by county roads, and on the top by a shelf of rock, a gift of the glacial age. How many miles wide was the park? I couldn't remember. A lot of miles.

The faintest echo of dogs barking and sirens screeching reached my ears. I shot a glance at Gino, waiting for him to finish his last set of instructions as cops, special agents, and private security firms banded together to create the world's largest perimeter lockdown. Wisconsin's largest, at any rate.

I stepped out of the car and pushed the seat up for Hector. Gino walked over to the most agitated-looking male in the center of the cop cluster. Establishing the order of the hunt. I shook my head and turned away from the uniformed cadre, scanning the hilly terrain around me. Gino could do the political thing. I'd left my last shred of patience on the auction barn floor, next to a few drops of my own blood. And an innocent dead man.

Nick and Gino's work was second to none. I knew any perimeter organized by them would be airtight—killer-tight even. But would this wildly diverse group of lawmen sharing their thoughts between country cell towers manage to get the park locked down fast enough to stop him?

There was only one way to find out. I rested my hand on the grip of my Glock, nestled in my shoulder holster. I patted my cell phone in my left pocket and clicked the radio transmitter clipped to the inside of my Packers' vest to make sure it was still live.

Hector stood behind me, breathing rapidly. I had no intention of waiting for the boys to decide who's who in the zoo. We didn't have that kind of time. I glanced back at Hector, cocking my head toward the edge of the forest. Then I turned and strode down into the ditch, long legs working hard to suck my feet up and out of the mud as I passed the abandoned truck. The breadcrumb trail of Burdock's prints beckoned me on.

CHAPTER TWENTY-TWO

The sound of Hector crashing through the dead leaves behind me reminded me of my last visit to the park, with a different olive-skinned man in hot pursuit. But we had been alone, in love, and about to take two very different life paths. I shook my head, lengthening my stride until we made it to the base of a steep embankment.

I stopped abruptly, staring at the ground and the surrounding trees and shrubs, looking for the telltale signs of human prey.

Hector's heavy breathing announced his arrival. "I thought you said there were dogs?"

I shrugged my shoulders without turning around. "I asked Gino if they'd ordered dogs. I'm guessing they did, thought I heard some, but we don't really know. And the longer we ..." A flash of silver-sided leaves in an ocean of chartreuse caught my eye. I pointed at a small opening in the face of the bluff and broke into a jog.

A sapling stood to the right of an old trailhead. My eyes followed the slender trunk to the earth. White rings of pressure where it had been forced aside feathered the base. "Here." I pushed into the forest and was relieved to find myself on a narrow game trail.

Who wouldn't take the quickest path out? Which, in this case, just happened to lead up. I turned my head toward Hector. "Call it in. He's on this trail."

I left him there with his radio crackling and plunged ahead into the lush shadows. The bluff was overrun with officers calling to one another and checking in on their radios. The sound of choppers drawing near overhead cushioned the din of the hunt. Still no dogs barking, no sounds of officers coming up behind me. *Where were they?*

The path cut sharply to the right, carving a trail that seemed nearly vertical. It rose above the pathways to a ridge that ran the length of the park. *You wanted to get above the fray, didn't you? Got a lookout point mapped out already? A hidey-hole maybe?*

I moved into a run as I drove myself up the path, grabbing trees and boulders along the way to propel myself along, concentrating on Burdock's mindset as I ran. *Yes. This is exactly where I'd go to hide.*

The earth was damp this deep inside the forest. The dank smell mixed with a sharper, acrid scent I couldn't identify. *Gasoline? No. Diesel fuel? Maybe.* I let the thought go and kept myself moving forward. Footprints rewarded my darting eyes every few strides. Sweat trickled down my back, and I pushed myself harder, faster, up the steep path, heading toward a landing about thirty feet from the top. I stopped at the landing, desperation flooding me, panting and sucking in deep breaths, unsure of my next move. Where was Hector? Gino? Where were the other officers?

Stones scuttled down the path in front of me. My eyes widened, and I fought the urge to turn and run screaming down the hill. Instead, I willed myself to freeze and look up, reaching for my Glock.

Guttural laughter trickled down from the ridge above me. The hairs on my arms rose. A large figure in a faded black duster stood directly in my line of sight.

The sound of tin ornaments clinking in the wind confused me as pressure filled my ears, leaving me dizzy and breathless, staring into the now empty incline. Where had he gone? Had

I even heard that noise? Had I really seen him? Or was this another trick of the mind, like tinnitus in overdrive?

I clenched my fists, ground my teeth and gave a growl before I realized it had escaped my lips. Glad to be alone, I holstered my Glock and reached for my radio. The mic wasn't on my vest anymore. My eyes dropped to the ground to check for it, and before I drew them back up to the trail, the eerie laughter floated down again. I wanted to stop and text the boys to let them know where we were, but the laughter was moving away from me.

I ran on ahead, with one hand tugging my cell phone from my back pocket, the other grabbing trees to steady my way. I stumbled on a root and fell to my knees, phone slamming to the ground as I instinctively broke my fall with both hands. I turned in time to watch as it bounced off a rock and slid down into a mound of leaves, thirty feet back down the trail I'd just climbed.

Crap. No time for this. I wheeled back around and resumed my ascent. A long, black coat traipsed on ahead, just out of reach, dancing between the shadows cast by low branches and boulders strewn along the trail. I pulled my Glock back out, steadied myself into a two-handed grip. "Stop! Police officer! Hands in the air—now!" Silence rippled down the path. I holstered the Glock and scuttled after him. Grabbing branches with both hands, I hoisted myself over a set of rock steps until I reached a small clearing.

Bracing myself against a pine trunk, I looked up and down the trail. Trees swayed in the wind, but nothing else moved. A black squirrel jumped noisily from one branch to another. I took a deep breath, steadying my shaky nerves. The fuel smell closed in around me. *Is it safe to fire my weapon?*

A twig snapped to my left, and I whirled around in time to see the hint of a black coat dart behind a tree about twenty feet beneath the clearing. I unholstered my Glock, raised it to shooting position and started down the embankment, training the gun on the base of the tree. "Come out with your hands on your head."

A whisper of black material flounced in the wind on the right side of the tree. *Gotcha, dirtbag.* "Come out from behind the tree. Hands on your head." At the sound of my voice, he moved farther behind the tree.

Was he going to make a run for it? Either way, he didn't seem too worried about my approach. Never a good sign.

I stood less than ten feet from the tree. Time to up the ante. "I'm giving you one last opportunity to come out with your hands on your head."

"I ... I can't," he answered in a string-tight baritone voice— the kind I would remember. But this voice was shaky as if laced with fear, nothing like the kind I would expect from the brazen man who'd eyed me on the other side of the window of The Pleased Pig.

A man peered from behind the tree, hands invisible from where I stood. He seemed to be kneeling, and his head was shaking uncontrollably. A black fedora toppled off his head, revealing thick, dark hair. Not the same man we'd been chasing in my stolen pickup all the way from Hillsboro. Not the same man at all. Not Alex Burdock but his friend Melvin White.

My mind struggled to comprehend what it meant that Melvin White crouched behind the tree, stuttering with fear. Where was Burdock? And what was up with White's odd movements? Was he stoned? Whatever he was on, I had to get him cuffed. I stepped toward him. The diesel smell was strongest near him, near the tree. *Did the gas leak when Burdock rolled the truck?*

I raised my Glock and focused on his eyes. "Here's how this goes. You put your hands behind your back, and you roll slowly back on your knees. You so much as twitch a muscle besides that, and I shoot you."

He looked up with soulful brown eyes. "I c-c-can't." His neck was taut. I followed the turn of his head, the awkward way it skimmed his shoulder.

"Perfect. Which leg would you like me to shoot?" I shifted my Glock, watching the words crawl through his mind. Something was wrong. Barks and the shouts of myriad officers drifted up from below.

Several long seconds later, he spoke again. "I c-c-can't." White-rimmed eyes glanced from me to the ground.

I studied him and the jerky movement of his neck. I drew my gaze down, seeing for the first time that what I'd taken for a part of the tree wasn't bark at all—it was the dusty black sleeve of his left arm, and it was laced with plastic ties to a logger chain. A quick scan of the other side confirmed it: someone had chained this man to the tree.

"What the … ?"

A whoosh of movement tickled my right ear. Followed by another. Heat kissed my neck. An arrow landed solidly in the middle of the tree, five feet from the ground. Red and yellow flames sputtered and went out. I watched in horror as the second arrow found its mark next to the man's left hand. The flames jumped from the arrow to the tree and raced upward. The man gasped. "T-too late."

I holstered my Glock, pulled out Nick's Leatherman and dropped to my knees in front of the bound man. I sawed against the thick plastic that held him to the chain, smoke billowing out as the tree started to burn. The man's hand clenched mine, stopping my sawing motion. A third flaming arrow hit him in the back. His eyes rolled up in his head, and he slumped over. I rocked back on my heels, jumped to my feet and tried to cut away the burning shaft, but the fire pushed me back. I took off my Packers vest and wrapped the fiery arrow in it, extinguishing the flames.

Flames whooshed up, surrounding the tree. The man's body stiffened. I looked down right before a nest of dry leaves at the base of the tree burst into flames. I couldn't catch my breath. Thick black smoke gushed against me. My shins were burning, and I could smell burned hair.

Screaming in frustration, I stepped back, impotent. The entire tree was in flames. Smoke gathered over the bound man's clothing. Tears blinded me, and I closed my eyes tight against the heat, still sawing away at the thick, unyielding plastic.

Accelerant. Not diesel fuel. We'd been Burdock's diversion. The cops would focus on us, easing up on the perimeter, thinking he was with me.

Burdock was getting away.

Voices drew near, and sharp canine whines drifted up from below. I gave another sawing push against the plastic bonds with the Leatherman, but the fire had accomplished what I couldn't. The bonds gave way, and my head banged against the tree. Pain flashed up my back. *Is my shirt on fire? No time.* White was slumped over. *Dead? Passed out? No time.*

Instinct took over, and I pulled him away from the tree, frantically searching for safety, a way out of the inferno. I could find none. I stopped, readjusting, facing White, grabbing his arms to pull again. My lungs burned as I sucked in the fiery air. Still, I dragged him, scrabbling backward through the flames, grateful for what I couldn't see. In the midst of my agony, God's voice rose above the roaring flames. *Forget what lies behind you. Reach forward to what lies ahead.*

Pull.

I shut my eyes against the heat and pulled. The skin on my arms quivered as flames jumped from the forest floor to my jacket. *Stop. Drop. And roll.* The din of cops and dogs and what might've been four-wheelers rose up to match the sound of the fire. For one quick second, I thought I was done.

I thought I was home. I opened my eyes, heat slapped against them, melting me. My hair was smoking.

This can't be how it ends.

White's body dug into the earth. I buried my head into the crook of my elbow, gasping, dragging in several large breaths of hot air through the fabric. Where were the guys? *No time. Pull.*

I channeled my freshman softball coach. I spread my legs shoulder-width apart, lowered my body, and leaned back, taut arms gripping under his arms. The only prayer I could think of rolled like a mantra through my mind. *Thy will be done. Thy will ... be done ... on earth ... as it is in heaven.* The image of a beautiful pair of hands reaching down from heaven, holding mine, as I pulled against White's weight was the last thing I remembered before sinking into darkness.

Antiseptic smells filled the air. A white noise backdrop heightened the beeping sounds of machines. My eyes were shut tight. It took all the strength I had to raise my lids to half-mast.

"And she's back." A male voice, thin with anxiety, carrying the hint of an accent.

"Ek ... tor?" Talking was a mistake. And judging from the confusion on the man's face standing over me, I might not, in reality, have been talking. *A big man, sporting a do-rag.*

"*Mija?*" *Not Hector. Gino.*

"Ino?" I wanted to ask him so much. But my brain and my lips weren't connecting. I stared up at him, willing all my words into my eyes, hoping he could read them.

"You are safe. That is the main thing." Gino's eyes were misty. The big softie. "And you somehow dragged Melvin White to safety. He lives. Though he is not free. He is in this hospital and under guard."

And Burdock? I wanted to ask. *Where's Burdock?* I looked up at Gino, concentrating on hardening my eyes.

"And Burdock—he hitchhiked off the mountain. Dressed in his Amish garb, what local wouldn't trust him? While every officer was racing up to the scene of the fire, he rushed away in a carjacked Buick, leaving the driver dazed, but alive, in his wake."

Why? Why kill the auction house man but not the driver?

"Who?" I did my best to croak my question, leaving it for Gino to decipher. Who'd he kill? Who were his latest victims?

"Hush, *mija*. Rest now. We'll talk when you awake." Gino stroked my forehead, brown eyes streaked with red, until I could no longer keep my own open and sleep took me.

CHAPTER TWENTY-THREE

Where was Nick? I woke again. Gino's face and every line spoke to me of kindness and of love. But where was Nick?

How could it be that I found myself once again in a hospital bed while he was out, only Nick-knew-where? *This cannot be happening again.* Where was he now? Was he safe?

Gino shook his head. His lips moved. *Silence.*

I squinted up at him, and the effort netted a flash of pain through both temples. I closed my eyes, trying to take a bodily inventory. All I knew was I still had one. And that it hurt. All over.

Scrunching my nose felt funny. I opened my eyes, aimed them down at my nose, and saw white. Bandages? Is that why I could barely hear Gino? I moved my head from side to side, pushing through the pain. One side didn't reach the pillow. Bandages.

I looked up at Gino, eyes moistening. "Nick?" *Where is he? Why isn't he here with me? Now, when I need him most?*

Gino bent down, closer to me. "Your Nick is out chasing the man who did this to you. And he will find him. But that is not your real question perhaps."

A thin smile broke across my face, stopping at the corner of the bandages around my nose. Fire, smoke, and the sensation of being dragged downward wisped through my mind.

"Nick." I breathed in deeply, held it in for several seconds, and slowly exhaled.

"Nick." The sound of his name rolled through me, fresh springs bubbling up from pristine tropical gardens.

"Nick." A profound sense of want, of desire, welled up inside me, vanquishing my long-held fears and doubts. *Perfect love casts out fear.*

"Your Nick has loved you for his whole life. He is a good man, Josephine—a great one. He would be a very good choice for you if you're asking for my opinion." He stroked my forehead. "This man is good for you, and he will make you very happy. If you're asking for my permission, this you have had since before you even needed it. I will tell you again: yes, Josephine. *Mija.* Marry him. Marry him, and do not look back."

I looked up at him. "Really?" Pain seared my throat.

"Really. Do not be afraid. Perfect love casts out all fear. And I would be so honored to be the one to give you away. If that is what you wish to ask next." He winked at me and gave a little tug on a lock of my hair.

I sighed, tears streaming silently down my face. Gino. My Gino. But how had he known to quote that same scripture? I smiled. God was in the house.

Sunbursts full of flowers danced across my mind. "Samantha." The action of the last twenty-four hours had left me little room to worry about my darling soon-to-be daughter.

"All is well with your leading ladies. I have checked on each of them for you." Gino tucked his hand into a jacket pocket and pulled out a picture. "And your mother is also fine. I called her myself to let her know that you are fine and could benefit from the prayers of a wise woman." He placed the picture on the tray in front of me.

Tears streamed down my face as I feasted my eyes on the picture of my mother and my Samantha and me. "Thanks, Gino."

"Nick has told me what Kira has done." He shook his head. "She will not succeed in keeping you and your girl apart. We will not let it happen. Rest, *mija*. You have done enough work for this day." Gino stood above me and sighed, gently wiping away my tears with a washcloth. A radiant smile transformed him from the black-ops tough guy to the soft-hearted saint he so often was in my life. My Cuban guardian angel stood over me like a sentinel.

God *was* in the house.

I closed my eyes, marveling at the stillness of my heart.

Nick.

I want Nick. Completely. The simplest revolutionary thought ever.

My eyes flew open, and I searched the hospital tray ahead of me for the framed picture Gino had left for me. It was my favorite picture of us, as Gino knew well. Me, holding Sam on my lap. My mother, nestled into me, chin resting on my head, arms around both me and Sam. I traced the beaded edges of the frame with my finger.

God, please bring Nick home to me, safe. Thank You for Your protection, for Your peace and Your guidance. Amen. Oh, and God? About that Nick-and-me business? All I can say is yes. Assuming it's Your will and all. Amen.

I held the picture to my heart, waves of pleasure surging through me. *Just need to Photoshop Nick in to complete my family.* Funny how much that little bit of talking and the power of my secret new truth drained what little energy I'd had upon awakening. Darkness reached toward me, and I closed my eyes once more.

Images of a barefoot Nick, clad in a black tux, shimmered in my mind. Samantha held his hand, laughing. She wore a flowy white dress, looking up at me, happier than I'd ever seen her. I said something simple to them both, with my mother standing by, all smiles, as the waves crashed in and pulled me under.

"Good morning, beautiful." Nick's silky tones drifted next to me as I lay in bed.

In bed with me? My eyes snapped open. Sharp stabs of pain hit from every direction. Oh. "Still here." I smiled up at him. *How long was I out?*

He leaned down, kissing me chastely on the cheek. "I can see that."

Purple half-moons were etched under his eyes. Dark stubble dotted his handsome face. "Oh, honey, you need rest. You should go." Where had he been? *Burdock!* "Did you catch him?"

He shook his head. "Not yet. But we're very close." Dejection pulled at his features, and I could see past the warmth to the emptiness in his eyes. *Failure. He's struggling with failure.*

He offered me his hand. I wrapped both of mine, bandages and all, around it. *Yeah. Me too, Nick. Me too.* I drew his hand to my lips, kissing each knuckle softly. "You really need some rest, hotshot."

"You see? Even she agrees." Gino's voice rose out of the corner of the room. How long had he been sitting there? *No wonder I feel so rested—these guys have my back. Again.*

Gino appeared at Nick's side. "Good morning, *mija*. You are looking well this morning, praise be to God. You will not mind if I take our Nicholas home for a few hours? He will not rest, nor leave your side without your word. I have assured him your kinsmen will take only the best of care of you."

"Kinsmen? Am I in Baraboo?"

Gino nodded. "When they found you, you had collapsed, overwhelmed by the smoke. You had freed the bad man's friend and were covering his body with yours as you passed out. You were *mija* to the end."

"And Burdock was probably already off Wildcat Mountain by the time they started dragging you away." The weariness in Nick's voice saddened me profoundly. What could I do to encourage this man?

I kissed the back of Nick's hand. "Go home and get some rest, handsome. I need you back by my side."

Nick's brown eyes were glistening as he squeezed my hand, bent down, kissed me on the forehead and whispered, "I love you, Josie."

Then he turned and walked away. Gino turned to me and winked before heading out the door behind him. I had almost faded back into sleep before I realized neither one of them had told me anything at all about the case. No doubt they wanted me to rest here for a few more days, but I was *not* about to sit this one out. I shook my head, willing myself to come to life.

Then I reached for the phone on the hospital tray in front of me.

"Josie! Where are you calling from?" The sound of Sheriff Tom Quinn's voice shredded what was left of my nerves. "I mean, should you be talking on the phone right now?"

"Come get me." I looked around my bed at the various machines and tubes, wondering which one to pull first and how much noise it would make. "I've just been released from the hospital."

Quinn was silent.

"We sent Nick home. He needs to rest. You sound fine. Now, come get me." If I didn't let him think about my request, he'd be more likely to agree. "See you in what, ten, fifteen minutes?" *Keep it moving. Keep him talking.*

"Thirty. Tops. I'm so glad you're well enough to be released. I got a very different picture from Nick ..." *Is that skepticism creeping in?*

"You know he can be a little melodramatic. Just come get me. Any updates on the case?" *Redirect him. Try to shift his focus off your growing line of little white lies.*

"You're not going to believe what we've pieced together. We're close, Josie, very close. Where will you be?" Eagerness replaced the skepticism.

"Meet me on the sidewalk out front. I'm going to get a little fresh air." *And if I make it off this floor without any alarms sounding, I'll need to stay away from lobbies and entrances.*

"I'll be there, Josie. In a company car."

"Great. Thank you, Quinn. I owe you one." I pumped as much normalcy as I could into my voice, and then I hung up.

Crap. Now what?

First things first. I drained the water glass in front of me, filled it, drained it again. *I can do all things through Him who strengthens me. I give You this day, this moment, this battle.* I tried to keep my prayers short in general. They tended to get really, really short when I might not be going straight by the book.

I shook my head, testing for dizziness. Then I sat up, swung my legs over the side of the bed and began the inventory. Both arms were bandaged to protect first- and second-degree burns, assuming I could trust my memory of the doctor's latest assessment. *Manageable.* My nose was still bandaged. *Not my best look.* More second-degree burns on both legs had been salved and dressed during my forty-eight-hour stay. *I could get pants on over those. Eventually.* Scorched hair that the nurses had delicately washed sometime in the past few hours tickled my fingertips. *Beauty school dropout.* No broken bones, mildly singed lungs. *Good to go, Jo.*

There was an IV line stuck in my right hand, clear liquid dripping slowly down. It didn't look all that essential to me. I turned the red clasp to stop the flow. Then I painstakingly—emphasis on the *pain*—pulled the tape off and yanked the needle out. Blood pulsed out, hitting the curtain and night stand. *Crap!* I grabbed the sheet and shoved it against my arm to stem the flow. The nurses made it look so easy! I unplugged the machine next to the bed, uncertain whether my handiwork would trigger an alarm.

Now what? I spied the wardrobe and stepped toward it. My body was stiff but not incapacitated. Thanks to the pain chaser, my limbs were itchy but not in agony. I could handle that. I found a couple of clean hospital gowns on the wardrobe shelf. The best I could do was wrap them around my backside in a makeshift outfit that wouldn't feature my bare butt as the main attraction. The loose cotton was probably all my tender skin could handle anyway. Quinn would just have to deal with my latest outfit. I'd gone AMA—Against Medical Advice—before. Sometimes just to avoid the lag time and paperwork. Getting into hospitals was easier than getting out of them, a lot easier.

I pulled myself to my feet, dull pain bristling along my singed skin. I took a deep breath and padded my way to the bathroom. Big mistake. My hair *was* relatively clean, but patches had been burned off, and the tape for the bandage over my right ear wrapped all the way around my head. Sort of like a headband. *I'll start a new trend.* The bandage on my nose was ringed with bruising—I didn't even want to think about what might be going on under there. I sighed.

I'm fine. Move out.

I pulled a pair of sunglasses from my purse, slid them on, and walked out into the hall.

And ran right into Nurse Ratchet.

CHAPTER TWENTY-FOUR

Lisa Bhatt gleamed from the smaller woman's bronze nametag. She had a regal bearing, one I associated with commanders of every stripe, and even before she said a word, I knew I'd been outgunned.

"Going somewhere, Chief?" Her smiling eyes didn't match her steely manner.

I sighed. "Look, I ..." I stopped, staring at her.

Her jet-black hair was pulled back into a tight bun. Lustrous cream-in-coffee skin was alive with energy.

I squinted at her nametag again. "Do I know you?"

"Hope so, Chief. Hop on. I'm your ride." Her light touch on my shoulder guided me into the wheelchair, and she didn't even wait for me to get settled in before pushing me smoothly toward the elevators, nodding curtly to a nurse who didn't look up as we passed her station. I watched as she hit the button for the third floor. A wave of dizziness washed over me as we swooshed upward.

Third floor? "Bhatt? Lisa? Wh ..." Talking hurt. "Where are we going?"

"We are engaging in community service." She pushed me out of the elevator and down the hall where two large men were standing guard. *White.*

"Brilliant." But what would we say to him? Beads of cold sweat formed at my hairline.

"Boys." Bhatt nodded at the armed tree trunks flanking the door.

They looked at her and nodded back. Trunk A unfolded his arms and stood aside while Trunk B scrambled to open the door. Job done, they finally noticed my bandaged body in the chair before them. Trunk A grimaced. "You catch the bastard that did this." Trunk B met my eyes, jabbed a thumb toward the open door. "He wasn't worth it, Chief. You're the bravest woman I know, and he wasn't worth it."

"We don't get to choose who's worth it. We just get to choose who we want to be today." I impressed myself.

Bhatt straightened. "Come on, Yoda." She gave the guards a final nod and pushed me into the room.

The mechanical whirring and thumping sounds in the room were a little louder than the white noise in my head. *White's arms tied to the tree.* Nausea rolled through me. *A flaming arrow snicking past my ear.* I clenched the wheelchair arms.

The man before me was swathed in bandages from the neck down. His right leg was in traction. His head was bandaged, and his face was slick with ointment. He tracked me with his eyes as Bhatt parked me next to the bed.

How bad were his burns? What happened to his leg? Did I do that? I tried to remember pulling him off Wildcat Mountain, but there was only blank space. I knew this was a powerful moment, but I couldn't think of anything to say.

Bhatt fidgeted. I held up a finger, silencing her before she spoke. Then I lifted my right arm painfully off the arm of the wheelchair, gestured to White and tried to cock my left thumb back at myself. "You wanna go to turnabout with me?"

White stared back at me, stupefied.

"No? Well, fine. We can still be friends. Let's just talk." So far, so good. But what was it I was trying to get out of him? A bottle of molasses gummed up my brain.

White's painkillers must've been better than mine. "Chief, you saved my life." His voice was weak but clear. "Thank you." He lifted a bandaged hand at me. "You risked your life, for me." His eyes glistened. "Why?"

"Because you are made in the image of God, and He loves you. And He isn't done with you yet." Where had that come from? "And because you are worth it, Melvin."

Compassion sprang from White's eyes like a fragrance. "After all I done? You got yourself close to killed, for me?" Tears fell down his cheeks. "I wanna make it up to you. Tell me what I gotta do. Anything, just, please ..." He was crying in earnest now.

Bhatt leaped in like a lioness. "You can tell us everything we need to know, that is what you can do." She pulled her cell phone from her pocket. "I will tape this conversation, is that okay with you?"

He nodded.

"You have the right to remain silent ..." Bhatt put a hand on my shoulder as she Mirandized him.

White continued weeping, unchecked. "I'm just so sorry. I never been worth nuthin', to nobody, till him ... but that was ... he was ... dirty."

I breathed in, feeling every microscopic movement. In a bad way. "But you are worth saving, Melvin. You are made in the image of God, and that makes you worth saving." Had I taken some sort of religious platitude drugs? Or was this the Holy Spirit finally having His way in my life? I hoped for the latter, fearing the former.

"But you saved me. After all I done ... I'm ... I'm sorry, Chief. Can you ever forgive me? I'm sorry." His eyes beseeched me.

And sent me into a rage. "For what? For this?" I pointed to myself. "Or for those people you murdered with your boyfriend?" Black smoke surged up my throat, and I was seized with the desire to smash him in the face. *Forgiveness? He wants forgiveness? He's a monster.*

Josephine, as I forgave you, so you forgive him. A rich voice filled my head with truth and my heart with peace.

Forgiveness? Obedience was all I could offer, forgiveness belongs only to God. To the One Most High, as I understand Him.

Obey. And give him your forgiveness. Now.

"White, I forgive you. Because He died so you might be made new. Even in this. Take that up with Him. But for me, yes, I forgive you." *I think.*

Lightness opened within me. I'd just done something good, something really big. Or else I was on one heckuva painkiller high. Time to press on. "White, how, why? Why those men? How did you two become a thing?"

I couldn't find the right words, I wasn't following any interviewing protocols, but he didn't seem to mind. "Chief, I …" A sob gasped from him. "We, there was no reason. We met in the FBI class."

Confirmed. "But why?"

He shook his head. "Weren't no why. Other'n the professor reminded Burdock of some bad days. And he's got some kind of power. Some kind of voodoo. He hooks ya in." His arms moved under the bandages, and his face glowed red under the shiny layer. "It was his idea. But he made it seem like mine." His voice trailed off.

Bhatt and I exchanged glances. "Where did you meet the victims—the men you murdered?" *So much for bedside manner.*

White started at *murdered.* "I, we—"

"We're not saying it's your fault, your idea, we—" Gray clouds swirling through my mind.

White nodded through it all, keeping his eyes only on me. "Chief, we, I …" Sorrow flooded his features. "It was like hunting. We set up an ad. An online ad. And I wrote it, mostly. And I called it 'Please Love Jesus and Huntin'.'"

"And will you give me your ID and password?" I was certain I could predict the physical preference section of the ad. "Did Burdock fill out the ad?"

White shook his head. "I done it myself. He give me ideas, but I done it myself."

"Did he give you ideas on how to describe the men you were looking for?" The chain of murders rolled out before me as White nodded. I didn't want to know any more, hear any more. Except for one thing. "What happened on Wildcat Mountain?"

White's face grew slack. "I dunno. We was luring you up top, to get to the professor. Burdock wanted him bad. He was my friend. We got tattoos. But then he turned on me."

"The professor?" Bhatt's voice broke the spell between us.

White nodded. "He wanted to kill the professor. From the day he seed him in class. Said he had to go where the all the others had gone."

Holy crap. Nick.

Bhatt thanked the men at the door and worked her magic at passing staff. We were through the lobby and heading to the parking lot in under three minutes. "Nice work, Bhatt."

"I should say the very same to you, Chief. And by the way, I texted Quinn about the tattoo. One of his nurse buddies will get back to us." She pulled out a key fob, pressed a button, and a cherry-red Bugatti roared to life. A Bugatti? In Baraboo, Wisconsin?

"You grow less forgettable by the half step, Bhatt." I thought back to when I'd met her, leaning over evidence at the crime scene on the sixth hole, smart and efficient. "Are you going to explain how and why you're here, or do I have to beg for it?"

She tucked me into the passenger seat like I was a child.

I rolled my eyes at her.

She smiled in response, humming, and got herself buckled in. She voice-texted the recorded confession to Amelia, Nick, and Quinn. Their names danced off the console screen like movie stars as she left a message of warning, repeating White's claims about Nick being the ultimate target. "Where were we? Ah, yes. First off, Sheriff Quinn was standing next to me when you called him. And, Sheriff Quinn being Sheriff Quinn, he sent me to fetch you instead. Secondly, well, I guess that's the end of the story." She pulled out of the parking lot. "Mind if we make a quick stop along the way?"

I stared at her. "Another one? Uh, sure. I guess. Is there a reason I should know about?"

"Have you *seen* yourself? No offense, but girlfriends don't let girlfriends go out looking like that. Especially not if they might be running into His Hotness."

"His Hotness?" I kept staring at her, eyes widening. "Do we have that kind of time? Have you heard back from anyone?"

She smiled, deftly handling the high-powered machine. "You know, Signore Vitarello, your love slave. And no, perhaps if you gave it thirty more seconds."

My mouth fell open, and still I stared at her. "Where are we going, and where have you been all my life?"

Her laughter was rich and beautiful. "Thank you for the compliment, Chief. We are stopping at my house, as we need to fix your face. I have more salve and fresh bandages to get you properly cared for—you know, in case your little AMA escapade leaves something to be desired in your burn-care program. Then, honestly, I would suggest a little makeup, and I have something in mind for your hair that might just work."

"Who *are* you?" This was a side of Bhatt I hadn't seen coming.

"Do not worry. I went to beauty school in a former life. And I am up-to-date on my first-aid training." She drummed her fingers lightly on the wheel.

We pulled into the driveway of a little Cape Cod, blue with white shutters and matching trim. "Home sweet home." She was at my door, helping me out of the car before I registered everything she'd just said.

"You are a force to be reckoned with, woman," was all I said as I followed her inside.

She turned and bowed before me, smiling, hands in prayer position. "Yes, I am. But not even half the force of the woman before me." She disappeared down a hallway, leaving me to wander through photographs on the wall and in frames on every flat surface. "And no word back yet from the Triumvirate. Or your Cuban godfather."

Gino. She'd texted Gino. I smiled.

The pictures documented a privileged youth. Lisa as a little girl wearing brightly colored saris, sparkling brown eyes full of life. Lisa as a teenager wearing a gown fit for a queen, bejeweled and surrounded by other beautiful girls. Riding a thoroughbred sidesaddle, dressed in hunt attire. I'd ridden most of my life and couldn't imagine sitting atop such a powerful beast, let alone jumping, in such an awkward position.

Who is this woman? And how did she end up in Baraboo, Wisconsin?

Bhatt returned bearing a makeup bag in one hand and a first-aid kit in the other. She gestured to a dining room chair. I pulled it out and sat down.

She handed me a glass of water before assuming her position behind my chair. "Drink up. Coffee's brewing. We must keep you hydrated. We'll start with your hair."

"Officer Lisa Bhatt," I said it slowly, drawing out each word. "You impressed me a few days ago—seems like two lifetimes ago. So, tell me your story. How does a rich girl from India end up in a small town in Wisconsin?" I waved my arm around the room at all her pictures.

She exhaled. "Oh. That. You really want to hear the story?"

I nodded slightly. "I do."

She resumed gently sifting through my hair.

"Well, it is a long one." Her accent rose, and her voice rose an octave or two. "First off, I am not from India. I'm from Pakistan. My father was—is—a wealthy Shiite." She snipped away at the bandages as she talked.

I nodded, not wanting to break the spell.

"As you can see, I was raised with privilege." She stiffened.

"I could get used to that." I was thinking of horses, dark chocolate, fresh fruit, and servants.

"No. You could not." She was pulling at my hair, cutting, teasing.

"Maybe not the sidesaddle part."

"And not the finishing schools or the very clearly defined, limiting and predetermined roles for men and women." She was pulling harder than necessary.

But I really wanted to hear more of her story. So, I said nothing.

"And though I've heard you know a little about bad marriages, I cannot explain to you the horror of the politically motivated marriage my father planned for me." She was cutting now, the whisking noises of the scissors punctuating her phrases.

"I was a very smart girl, which is nothing to be proud of among some members of my family. And I was, in the eyes of my people, most desirable." The snipping had finished—she was fluffing and examining her work now.

"You're a beautiful woman, pretty sure that's how any culture would see it." How had she gone from the life of privilege in the photos to an American beauty school?

"But I wanted to be known for more. I wanted my life to count for something, for justice." The impact of her words jarred me. "But to my father, my life mattered only as a business venture. He arranged my marriage to a very wealthy, very powerful, and very bad man."

She stepped away from my chair for a second, admiring her work. "And I had other plans for myself. So, I fled my country and my family. And got as far away as I possibly could. I went to a place no one would ever think to look for me." She put the scissors down on the table and retreated into the kitchen.

Lisa Bhatt wanted to make a difference with her life. She wanted to live for something bigger than herself—she wanted her life to *count*.

She was just like me. And she'd also paid a high price for her freedom. I decided then and there, she and I would be friends for life. The cherry-red Bugatti was icing on the cake.

Between styling what was left of my charred hair and applying what makeup she could to my injured face, Officer Bhatt told me bits and pieces of her story. Nothing could top the kicker of her being a real live Pakistani celebrity—though the harrowing emigration to get away from a power-crazy fiancé took a close second. *Talk about your escape to Wisconsin ...*

Thirty minutes later, we were back on the road, fresh coffee in travel mugs and a brand-new attitude electrifying the air around us. C. S. Lewis and I shared the belief that friends unite around one simple question—*do we see the same truth?* From everything I'd heard, Officer Bhatt and I were cut from the same cloth.

"How good a shooter are you?"

She turned to me, one eyebrow lifted and grinned. "I get by."

"You got enough room in this thing for guns and ammo?"

"I never leave home without them." She kept her eyes on the road, composed as a celebrity. "And yes, I have an extra

Glock for you, since Hector took yours away at the scene. Or if you prefer a high-powered rifle, I have that as well. And I always pack a few knives. And a Barretta over-under, just in case."

I nodded, lips pursed in admiration. "You got anything more interesting than what we're about to hear from the Feds?"

Bhatt shook her head, kicking her dream machine up over eighty in silence.

Admiring the feel of the sleek machine, I kept my musings to myself. They couldn't have any new leads. Otherwise, Nick would've never agreed to go back to the hotel with Gino to catch a few zees. I prayed to God to heat up the trail. We had to catch this guy. Now, before …

"You have a call, Madame." I jumped in my seat as a masculine English accent filled the car.

Bhatt laughed. "Relax, farm girl." She pushed a button with her thumb. "Bhatt."

"Lisa, is Jo with you?" Quinn's voice was so clear, I expected to see him pop around her seat.

"Affirmative, sir." Bhatt looked at me, rolling her eyes.

"Good. Meet me in Merrimac. At the ferry."

"Sir?" Bhatt grimaced and let up on the gas.

"You heard me." Quinn's voice was clipped.

There had to be a break in the case. But why was he calling us? He'd sent Bhatt to pick me up, thinking I was good to go. *Thought he knew me better than that.*

"Roger that." Bhatt slowed the car to around thirty, checking her rearview mirror every few seconds.

"What's going on, Quinn?" The suspense was killing me. Before I could say another word, Bhatt manhandled the car into a U-turn without slowing down. I grabbed the handhold and clamped down a scream.

The squeal of the tires rolled around us, and acrid air filled the car. Black smoke puffed up behind us, and I couldn't help it … I yelped.

"Should you be doing this, Josie?" Concern laced Quinn's voice.

"How'd you know it was me and not Bhatt squealing?" I looked over at her and winked.

"You don't know Bhatt." Quinn ended the call.

She tossed me a wicked grin and hit the gas.

CHAPTER TWENTY-FIVE

Bhatt wheeled her sleek machine into an angled parking slot next to Quinn's SUV. One looked as out of place as the other in front of the battered wooden dock extending over the Wisconsin River. I watched the waves chop over the rocks as I heaved myself out of the little car.

"Be easier to get out of a Big Wheel. How do you *do* this every day?"

"You don't know Bhatt." Quinn's voice boomed over the sound of the waves.

I turned around to find him steps away from me, his approach rendered soundless by the wind and the crashing of the river.

Bhatt rounded the front of the car, and we both leaned in closer to Quinn.

"What's up, boss?" Bhatt handed him the conversational ball.

"We think he's here." Quinn looked out at the churning water.

"On the river?" I stopped short in front of the three-point line.

"Yup. On the water." Quinn kept staring at the river.

"But how do we know it's him?" Bhatt asked.

"We're not a hundred percent sure, but we've got some grainy images from a farmer's drone that look pretty promising."

"Excellent." Bhatt started snapping up her jacket.

"Wait. *Farmers* have *drones*?" Lots had changed since I'd left home.

Bhatt and Quinn shared a look.

She rolled her eyes at me. "Everyone's a drone out here. Not the point. Go on, boss."

"He's ditched the Amish look, cut and colored his hair, but the facial recognition software puts him at a seventy-some percent probability for Burdock. And he's become sloppy. Nick says forensics is having a field day with the evidence he's left behind." Quinn thumbed through his cell phone.

"Sounds close enough for government work. What's the plan, boss?" Bhatt was powering up. Energy practically surged out of her.

I looked around. "Where are the Feds? Nick on his way? Want me to text Gino?" There were no other cop cars to be seen, marked or otherwise.

Quinn and Bhatt looked at each other again.

Quinn cleared his throat. "I'm heading this piece of the hunt. Rivers are what I do best. The Feds are a little tied up at the moment. Last I heard, Nick and Gino were catching a little R and R after chasing down leads at a rural airport near Madison most of the night. Besides, they're not really water boys."

I stared at him, eyes narrowed. "This wouldn't have anything to do with your relationship with Nick, now would it?" I'd never known him to be petty, but competition could bring out the best or the worst in a person. "And isn't this case already squarely FBI? Come to think of it, the river runs through several states, right?"

"Yes. Well, not entirely. The river is in Wisconsin. As such, the Department of Natural Resources is also involved." The finality in his tone surprised me. Until I remembered his brother being named to the top DNR post in the state a few years ago.

I decided to go for it. "But I thought *you* were the one who called Nick into this case to begin with."

He avoided my gaze. "Yeah. I did."

"I thought that's what you wanted—to team up with the FBI."

"So did I." Lines of tension creased his jaw. "But Nick wasn't all that excited about my seventy-some percent drone sighting. And I am. This feels right to me." He turned away from us toward two kayaks fastened to the top of his SUV. White-stenciled letters marked them as Property of the Sheriff's Department. He started unbuckling the straps.

I watched in silence, the muscles at the base of my neck forming angry knots. One of the kayaks was a one-seater. The other had room for two.

Bhatt coughed behind me.

I turned around to face her. "What?"

"I call shotgun."

Quinn eased the kayak gear onto the ground. He then started a quick but methodical check of each piece of equipment. I was going to give him a piece of my mind but thought it better to let him finish checking the equipment first. Then I'd lay into him.

Bhatt tugged at my sleeve and grabbed my elbow. I winced as fire ants bit into my arm from the inside out. I breathed deeply, counted to ten, let it out. Then I let her guide me back to the driver's side of her car.

"You okay, Chief?" Her almond eyes were alive with worry. I nodded.

She glanced over her shoulder at Quinn, still dutifully prepping our rides. "While the boss finishes looking over the equipment, give me a quick primer on the fine art of kayaking." Her face had turned a light cream color. Was she afraid of the river?

"Oh, c'mon, Bhatt! Didn't they teach you how to kayak in finishing school?"

She stamped her boot on the gravel. "Just shut up and teach me."

I hoped the foot stamping had been involuntary. I decided to let it slide. "It's easy, really. You ever been in a canoe?"

Her cheeks deepened to a taupe color. "Not really."

I winced. "A rowboat?"

She shook her head.

"What watercraft have you been on? Let's start there." I was getting a slight fluttering in my gut.

"You probably do not want me to describe my father's many yachts. Or how sailing never required my personal attendance to physical details of any sort." Indignation covered her embarrassment as she spat the words out.

"How'd you get through the sheriff's department training program without spending any time on the water?" I placed a hand on my hip and shifted my weight. And winced.

"I told you. I am an excellent marksman. My skills lie in other domains." Her words were clipped.

"Oh, for Pete's sake. That why you want to ride shotgun?" A plan formed in my mind. I looked her up and down, guessing I had a good twenty pounds on her, hopefully not thirty.

"Yes, in the worst possible way. It doesn't look too difficult. I am sure I can manage with your help." Her tone shifted from schoolgirl back to cop. I liked cop better on her.

I took a deep breath, let it out. "Fine. C'mon, let's go see what Quinn's got in mind."

We walked back to Quinn's SUV just as he was finishing up the equipment check. I knew from experience he'd done the same thing before ever packing it up, remembering how his need to measure twice and cut once had saved my butt on more than one occasion when we'd gone on river outings in high school. He stood up and stretched as we approached, thumbing through his cell phone and sending another text.

I made a snap decision while he was texting, and I turned on my phone's recorder. Something about the way he'd invited Nick into the fray only to shut him out as we were possibly closing in on Burdock felt wrong to me. I was the last person to pass judgment on someone else's passions driving their actions. But, I didn't want his jealousy standing between me and the rest of my life.

"So, a drone sends you river intel, says it got the drop on the bad guy, then tells you to put in at the Merrimac Ferry?" I cut to the chase.

"Drone and satellite images show a man matching Burdock's general description in a flat-bottomed canoe a good twenty miles upriver from here. Conventional wisdom suggests the best way to catch a fish is with the right kind of bait."

Red heat flamed up my neck. "We're your bait?"

Bhatt shrugged. "We're all we've got."

"And it helps if, in addition to being close enough to the right kind of bait, you just happen to have a big net and a faster boat." Quinn looked at us as if to gauge the effect his crazy-making had on us. "The bait has already been set. A series of fake police radio transmissions are being sent out right now, making it sound as if Nick himself is in pursuit of the suspect somewhere between Reedsburg and LaValle. Dixon thinks a river escape falls within the realm of the possible, but she's keeping her units on the roads. Figures it keeps up the charade on their end while leaving us free to set the trap on ours. That should lull Burdock into enough security to do whatever it is he plans to on the river today. If it is him. Given his history with White, a river kayak makes as much sense as continuing on the roads."

"And we will be there to scoop him into our net." Bhatt tapped her boot heel. "Not bad, Boss. Not bad at all."

I nodded my head. "If he *is* planning a river escapade, we'll throw him a nice surprise party. Your little river cruise idea could actually work." Especially with a good old Cuban-American backup plan. I turned my body away from them, stopped recording and sent the plan to Gino.

Quinn hefted his kayak above his head and started toward the river's edge. I pawed through the pack he'd left for us until I found the life vests. I tossed one absentmindedly to Bhatt. "Put this on, oh celebrity."

She scurried over to me, dark thunderclouds roiling in her eyes. "Do not call me that!"

"Relax. Quinn's practically deaf as a stump. Besides, you *are* a celebrity."

"Exactly the point." She hissed at me through clenched teeth, snapping the vest into place. "Not anymore."

"That why you drive a two-million-dollar car?" I winked at her. "Less chatter, more heavy matter. Help me lift this thing."

I tossed the pack to her, breathing deeply while she threw it over her shoulder. I waited for her nod before lifting the front end of the kayak off the ground. She was a quick study. She grabbed her end, and together we lifted the craft up onto our shoulders. Pain bolted through me as I lifted my arms over my head. Each footstep sent fresh waves of agony up and down my body. My arms were shaking when we finally reached the rocks just in time to watch Quinn navigate a patch of sand between them. He rested while we caught up to him. My skin burned underneath my bandages, fresh blisters popping. I didn't want to think about what lay ahead.

Samantha. Hair flying in the wind. Smile bright as the sun.

I looked up at Quinn. "So how exactly is us being here, him being up there, going to result in us actually catching him?" In spite of what I had said aloud for Gino's benefit, I had turned Quinn's strategy over in my mind during the portage. So far, I had nothing.

Bhatt joined in. "And why in the world would he be on the river in the first place?"

Her question, I could answer. "Because all the roads are blocked. And no cop worth her salt is going to let him slip through the woods again. I'm liking the river route more every time we talk about it. Guy like that has to have given himself more than one escape route. At least, I hope so. Might drown himself, save us the trouble." I thought of the tricky underwater currents that took people under every single year. The power of the Wisconsin River demanded respect. Would he understand that much? Did he have the upper body strength to match the river or skills as wily as hers? For that matter, did Bhatt? Could I make it with my battered body? Only time would tell.

"Smart money says he's hedging his bets, hoping to make it to the busy stretch between Spring Green and Prairie du Chien. If he takes the bait, that should put him in the water heading our way right about now. Dixon concurs. Burdock's heading south." He turned away from the river, focusing on me.

"Wouldn't be the worst plan in the world, though he'd have to be a heckuva sportsman to make it that far, spring river and all." Recently melted snow made the currents all the stronger. "Then what? Boost a car, jump the line into Iowa or back into the flatlands of Illinois maybe?"

"Something like that."

I looked from him to Bhatt. "I'm assuming you guys have roadblocks set in place just in case, right?"

"Aye, aye, Chief." Bhatt nodded at me. "Right, Sheriff?"

Quinn nodded, phone buzzing. He pulled up a text, read it and jolted upright. "Fresh batch of drone photos from my friend at the Farm Bureau suggests he might've just put in a few miles north of here. It's go time. Saddle up."

CHAPTER TWENTY-SIX

"Okay, Bhatt. We're lowering the kayak into the water, and I'll turn it around so you can get in easier as I walk into the river. You're going to wait until most of it is in the water. I'll keep her steady and wait for you."

Bhatt nodded grimly. Quinn was already afloat.

I winked at her, faced the river and strode quickly into the swirling waters, bracing myself for the frigid reception. It didn't help. Icy fingers of water tore at my clothing and soaked my bandages. I gasped, letting the shocking waves roll over my legs. Everything was playing out as planned, up until the point where Bhatt was supposed to follow me into the river. I faced her, holding the bucking kayak in place and beckoned her in.

Her eyes were rimmed with white, and for a moment, I was sure she'd bolt. She swallowed, looking at me like a terrified fawn.

"Move, Bhatt! One foot in front of the other." I shoved the kayak as close to the bank as I could, edging it onto the sand. "You don't even have to get in the water. Just get in. I'll do the heavy lifting from back here. Move to the side of the kayak, put your butt in the seat and pull your legs in."

What her wooden movements lacked in grace, they made up for in speed. She was in her seat before I could worry about her. I jumped into mine, glad to get my legs into the relative warmth of the air.

I jabbed my paddle into the river, pulling us around to follow Quinn, who bobbed in the distance. "Just like I told you on land. One smooth stroke down through the water on one side, lift it up and do the same on the other side. I'll talk you through it and do all the steering."

Bhatt's back was rigid, making her movements in and out of the water stiff and her shallow paddling as much a hindrance as a help. I countered her jerky movements with my own strong, smooth, deep strokes, muscle memory kicking in as my wounds shouted out, alternating on either side of the kayak.

A gray shape jutted out of the water, fifty feet ahead of her. "Bhatt! Paddle left. Left! The *other* left!"

I stuck my paddle deep into the water on the right side of the boat and kept it there, counting on her frantic paddling to help swing us around. Seconds later, the big river rock sailed past on our right. I exhaled, long and loud, and kept paddling.

"Why did you not tell me about the rocks?" Bhatt's accent sharpened as she paddled.

"You can go back to alternating sides with the paddle now. And slow your roll. Paddle smooth and steady." I looked upriver at Quinn, bent over his cell phone, frantically poking at the screen, as I steadied our little craft. What had he learned?

Bhatt would paddle once, maybe twice, then her fear would crawl up her spine, causing her weight to shift and the kayak to move with her. Her panic was endangering us both. I had to talk her off the ledge, or she'd put us both in the water— maybe worse.

"Listen, Bhatt, Lisa, you got this. Just relax, breathe, and slowly paddle on one side of the kayak and then the other. It's easy."

"I do *not* have this, Chief." She kept her frantic paddling up.

Another large rock appeared on our right, less than thirty feet ahead. "Bhatt. Relax. Put your paddle on the right side of the kayak and paddle faster."

She looked up. And panicked. She jumped out of her seat like a cat, landing too far to the left.

"Bhatt! Stop it! Calm down!" My shouting only panicked her more. *Time to try a different approach.*

She looked back at me, terrified. "Do you have any more fine advice?"

"Yeah. Not sure how all this works on your side of the ocean and all, but feel free to start praying, fasting and maybe sacrificing small woodland animals at any time."

"You are a cretin!"

"Yeah, I get that a lot."

I opened my mouth to tell her how to steer away from the rocks when she screamed and leaned her weight too far to the right.

"Relax, Bhatt. We got this." I spoke in low tones, trying to calm the wild animal that had been unleashed inside her. And then I saw what she saw—five feet of glistening charcoal shale jutted up in front of the kayak, slightly to our right.

"Hard right! Paddle hard right!" I jabbed my paddle into the swirling waters trying to steer us away from the rocks. For a moment, I thought we might sneak past it.

But I couldn't control Bhatt. She panicked again, overcorrected, lost her balance, flew to the right of the kayak, then leaped back to the left. The kayak bucked and shifted. The rocks moved toward us at the speed of sound, and we crashed right into the hulking mass of rock.

The hull of the kayak moaned and split open. Water rushed in, covering Bhatt's feet, her legs. I was about to tell her how to lower herself safely into the rapids, when a wall of water slammed into us from the side, pushing us into the middle of a wild cauldron of churning waters.

My head snapped to the left and back again, hard. Cracking sounds reverberated up and down my neck. Was it broken? My end of the kayak slammed into another rocky outcropping.

Pain shot through my shoulder, and then my head followed the movement, smacking hard against the rocks. An image of Bhatt throwing her paddle into the air and jumping into the foaming waters was the last thing I saw before everything went black.

A thousand scorpions stinging me to death. A giant, out-of-control washing machine tearing me one way, dragging me another. A steel sword jamming into my thigh, and a concrete wall slamming me from the back. Teeth chattering. Cold blasts of air pulling through me. A giant's wings fluttered above.

Sunlight seeped through my slitted lids as I slowly opened my eyes. Nausea churned through me. I turned my head and emptied the contents of my stomach onto the ground next to me. I bolted upright, wanting to get as far away from the foul liquid as possible. My head burst into a red ball of pain. I leaned back on my arms and breathed deeply.

"She is awake. *Mija*, I am here."

Cuban cigars, fresh linen, applewood bacon, strong arms pulling me into safety.

"Gino!" I wrapped my arms around him, burying my head into his chest. "But how?"

"Your foresight in sharing Quinn's plan has saved your lives. It is that simple." Gino smoothed my forehead. "The moment I received your message, I followed your signal. And so it is, we found you both."

"Bhatt?" I could only hope she'd made it out of the river alive and with all her parts intact. Gino's light tone suggested as much.

"The lovely Officer Bhatt is changing into dry clothes." *Thank God.* "And she credits you with her rescue, the timing of your text."

"Timing is everything, G." I pushed away from my muscular friend.

Zaps of pain flooded me, and I touched a soft spot on my forehead gingerly. Jackhammering sensations pounded my temples as I completed my inspection. A goose egg on the back of my head, the smaller one on my forehead and an open gash near where the bandage used to be had been added to my injuries. *Great.*

"Where's Burdock? And Nick? Did you bring him?"

He pressed four pills into my hand, passing me an opened bottle of water. "Extra-strength ibuprofen. It's all we've got for the moment. And know that our Nick has a mind of his own. Once we had pulled you to safety, he insisted on joining Quinn in pursuit of our suspect—who is believed to be farther down the river."

Had he floated past us? I slammed the ibuprofen down with a long slug of water. "Quinn and Nick on the river together, teaming up again? Oh boy." After I'd gone behind Quinn's back and called in my own cavalry? *Oh boy.*

"Yes. Knowing our boys as we do, I imagine their wild river ride could rival any memorable scene from *Deliverance.*" Gino's matter-of-fact tone did me in.

I spit out a sip of water and collapsed into laughter, then grimaced as spasms of pain jabbed into my ribs.

Bhatt appeared, wearing dry clothes, and launched immediately into a fair rendition of that infamous tune. Her mouth-harping the *Deliverance* theme was so completely out of character Gino and I crumpled back into shrieks of laughter. Tears squeaked out of my eyes, and I looked up at her with renewed admiration, our near watery death notwithstanding.

She held a bundle of clothes out to me. "Here, put these on." She placed them on the ground in front of me, then retreated half a step.

I looked at the clothes, then back up at her. "I know you didn't have these with you in the kayak."

Her eyes sparkled. "Your friend is very perceptive. And inventive." She turned aside and gestured behind her.

In the clearing beyond where we rested sat Bhatt's little red gem. The Bugatti glittered on the other side of a sea of bright green leaves. I marveled at her perfect lines and turned to Gino. "How'd you get the thing started?"

Gino and Bhatt exchanged a glance. "I don't want to hear this again," Bhatt said. "All I know is my baby is in beautiful shape, and she is right here when we need her. And like you, I've learned to come to the party prepared." She nudged a toe at the tidy pile of clothes on the ground next to me. A white box with a red cross sat next to it.

"Well-played, G. Well-played." I smiled, images of Gino breaking into and hotwiring Bhatt's two-million-dollar beauty dancing through my head.

Inch by painful inch, with Bhatt's careful assistance, I managed to change out of my heavy, wet clothes and wrap the scratchy blankets around me. The river had wreaked havoc with my bandages, and Bhatt's little white box had just what the doctor ordered in that department too. "Of course I keep a well-stocked first-aid kit in my primary vehicle. Doesn't every cop?" She seemed miffed at my surprise.

I thought of my tin lunch box sporting a picture of Dale Evans, Roy Rogers, and Trigger and its meager supplies of Barbie Band-Aids and bacitracin. "Yeah, sure."

She was as careful with my burns as she had been earlier, gently rubbing them with some mystery salve that dialed back the pain several notches the minute after she applied it. Then she wrapped my legs, arms, nose, and ear back up.

She appraised her work when she finished, then handed me the small pile of clothes. "You'll feel better when you change into dry clothes." She walked over to her car to join Gino. A small group of officers from the Sauk County Sheriff's Department stood around them. She peered over Gino's shoulder at a piece of paper he had been reading out loud.

I dressed and began the slow walk to the little group. Gino had said he drove Bhatt's car to the ferry with Nick following in Gino's Z28. Given Nick's quick exodus to join Quinn on the river in another sheriff's-department one-seater, that left the three of us with two cars. I had an idea where we might be headed.

I wanted to make sure my two amigos were on the same path. "Head to Prairie du Chien? Beat them to the trailhead?" *I'm going to need a few more pills.*

Gino nodded slowly. "That is my thinking." He stepped away from the group of chinos-clad men, folding a piece of paper into his pocket and beckoned us to follow. "I think we leave these gentlemen here to make sure the *malo* doesn't double back, and we take our show on the road."

"So, we all go to Prairie du Chien?" I didn't want to leave it to chance. Woozy sensations floated over me.

"Yes." Bhatt and Gino chorused. *Had they talked it over without me?*

I was in no shape to drive and chose to join Bhatt for the ride. I had every intention of teaching her better ways of navigating churning waters by way of regaling her with river stories, but I was asleep the minute the smooth engine purred to life.

CHAPTER TWENTY-SEVEN

A change in speed woke me up. Bhatt downshifted as we passed a rickety sign sporting a white, hand-painted greeting: Welcome to Prairie du Chien.

"Prairie of the dog? As in prairie dogs? What kind of name is that to give a booming metropolis like this?" Bhatt's mood behind the wheel of her Bugatti was a solid improvement over her mood behind the paddle of a kayak. I kept that observation to myself.

"Turn right at that stump. See the dirt road up ahead?" I pointed down the road unnecessarily.

"The one adjacent to the lovely Guppy's Minnows and Other Bait Shoppe?" She pointed a sleek, manicured finger at a dilapidated storefront.

"That's the one."

"And is that a surname, Guppy?" She was back. Snippy even.

I smiled. "Yup. Though I wouldn't call ol' Gup *sir*. No siree."

She turned onto the dirt road as directed, tsking as dust rose over her beautiful ride. I rolled my eyes. "Just park it. You can wash it later. On second thought, maybe you should hit the road, join Gino at the trailhead, make sure Burdock doesn't get past us."

She squinted at the shack before us. "I will not leave you here alone. Freshen up, I'll wait."

I smiled. "Awww. Thanks, Mom. But I'm fine. Really. Just hand me a five spot before you go and then head on up the road. With you and Gino scouting the local stops, you both ought to be back here before I finish."

She looked at me, eyebrows arched.

"I'm going to go in, mix with the locals. Ask a few questions. Always looks more legit if you buy something. And I'll make up a story about you abandoning me here, cover for your impossible ride showing up in a dump like this."

She handed me the money. Her phone buzzed. "Wait a minute. Gino's texting." She read her phone and looked up at me. "White's tattoo. It was another letter. An *S*." I'd forgotten all about it. "An *S*? So that gives us, what, a game of Scrabble gone bad?"

Bhatt gave an impatient shake of her head. "Gino seems to think the letters may have been an address. A street name even."

"What?" I squinted at her. Squinting didn't seem to hurt.

"The letters. *J-E-M-E-H-A-I-S*. What if they are a partial street name out in the middle of nowhere? Wisconsin's colorful past includes some settlers from all over the world. This area is full of unusual names of Native American Indian, French, and Spanish, Scottish, even Asian origins." Bhatt's recitation sparked my memory.

"Well, we grew up on some pretty grim tales about traders and merchants of old, and it's true, they had to get through Prairie du Chien to get to the rest of the world. At one time, it was the largest trading post in the territories." Pictures of large bearded men laden with pelts and weapons danced through my mind. "You got any paper, a pen in this jalopy?"

Bhatt opened a console I hadn't noticed between us and pulled out a small notebook, pencil tucked on top. "Work your magic."

I wrote out the letters. "*J-E-M-E-H-A-I-S*." I studied it and recalled the *M* and *E* had appeared on the same bead. I circled the pair, trying different pronunciations. "Gem hays? Gee me hah ..." My voice trailed off as knowledge washed over me. "Holy crap. Not an address. A phrase. In French."

"What?" Bhatt took the notebook from me. "French? 'I hate myself'?"

"Yes. *Je me hais*. He's telling us the men, Nick, they have no value. They are all substitutes for his abuser, and he hates them, making them the perfect victims." *Nick*. "Bhatt—you've got to go. Now. Catch up to Gino, and between the two of you, bring my Nick back safe."

"Don't worry Josephine—we will find him." Her eyes glistened.

Patting empty pockets in search of my cell phone, I sighed. It was probably on the bottom of the river. "Find him." My words came out in a whisper. I hefted myself painfully out of her car.

I watched as she rolled slowly away, then I limped into the bait shop.

Nick. He has to be okay. Please, God. I pushed the thought he might not be out of my mind, willing my limp to fade as I walked. With every step, my hunger and thirst magnified, until it was official: I was jonesing for a bag of BBQ Corn Nuts and an ice-cold can of Diet Coke. A glass door, littered with flyers taped to the inside, sported a list of offerings, hand painted in splotchy red lettering. In my exhaustion, I could have sworn they were painted in blood. LIQUOR MALTS FIREWOOD SNACKS FLIES NIGHTCRAWLERS MINNOWS GRUBS ICE BUT NO GUPPIES.

I shook my head. Only in Wisconsin. And maybe on the set of *Fargo*. Pushing my way inside, I lost my balance in the darkness. I reached out for a nearby shelf, hoping to steady myself, and managed to knock over two rows of canned goods instead. *Smooth.* They scattered to the floor, announcing my arrival to the nonexistent customers in the crammed little shop. Once my eyes adjusted, I picked up the cans.

The shop was a glorified box. Each side had windows running along the top, air holes really, complete with dirty gingham curtains, remnants of the owner's one and only long-term relationship. There were two interior aisles of groceries and "assorted home goods," according to a small sign atop one of the rows. The back of the shop featured water tanks, and I knew from past visits the tanks would be full of bait, as advertised. A strange assortment of camping and canoe equipment and hardware supplies lined one wall.

A purveyor of curiosities, Gup could outfit yuppies for a river trip or cater to rednecks looking for nothing more than a six-pack and a carton of nightcrawlers. Opposite the wall full of hammers, shovels, and who knew what all was Guppy's little office. Guppy himself spent much of his life glued to an old stool with a duct-taped vinyl cover, in front of a cigarette-smoke-stained counter, attached to an old-time cash register.

He sat there now, looking at me without blinking.

"Afternoon, Gup." I nodded my head at him, keeping my distance, letting him lead the dance.

"Miss." While he did nod back at me, he otherwise didn't move a muscle. His arms were crossed over his aging frame, and his dark brown curly hair framed a pair of brown eyes that were rimmed in red. *Allergies?*

"You gotta phone I could use?" I had to call Nick, hear his voice. *Please let him be okay, God.*

Gup shook his head.

I waited for him to say something, scanning my brain for any recent feuds between his kin and mine. Finding none I could remember, I shrugged my shoulders and headed toward the snack rack standing in front of the tanks.

A long wooden pole that had once held a shovel had been run through the hard plastic handles of each tank. Gup's makeshift security system, designed to keep kids and tourists from leaving the tops off. I turned to face him.

His eyes widened in alarm. "Where ya going there, missy? Ain't nothin' there for the likes a you. We fresh outta your favorites."

"Gup." I soothed. "Don't be rude. I can see them from here." Five shiny new bags of BBQ Corn Nuts gleamed at me. While I couldn't see the expiration date from here, I had a good feeling about them.

I stopped in front of the rack and snapped off two bags of the beauties. "I'm just gonna grab myself a Diet Coke from the cooler in the back." *Anything to distract myself from the fire ant worries chewing through every nerve over Nick.*

Something in Gup's expression sent mild waves of alarm through me, but they rolled into the waves of pain, swirling into a big gray, diaphanous wall in my mind. Gup grunted something, but I couldn't quite make it out. I blinked, shook my head to clear it. *Mistake.* I waited for the pain to clear, noticing for the first time that Gup reminded me of someone, but I couldn't put a name to the person. Actor? Musician? Two hallways stood in front of me, waxing and waning as if I stood before a funhouse mirror. Once the pain subsided to a dull roar, I stepped to the right, into a narrow hallway. Barreling past the bathroom I remembered for its questionable cleanliness, I headed toward a refrigerator with an old-time metal handle. I could almost taste that ice-cold cola running down my parched throat.

I pushed through a curtain of beads hung decades ago by Gup's former wife and found myself face to face with an angry-eyed man with freshly dyed hair. *Burdock.*

He was taller than he'd looked through the plate glass of The Pleased Pig two days ago in Reedsburg, with muscular arms emphasized by the rolled-up sleeves of a plaid flannel shirt. The tag still dangled from the collar. The look was a far cry from Amish farmer or nerdy professor. I missed the bowtie.

His icy blue eyes hardened. *So much for skating past him and quietly calling it in.* "Nice shirt. Should I add shoplifting to your ever-expanding list of crimes and misdemeanors?" My smart mouth had been a problem since first grade. *Too late to rein it in now.*

He looked me up and down. *Trying to intimidate me, or wondering if I'm armed?* It gave me just enough time to take a half step back and drive my knee into his groin. The unexpected blow knocked him backward into the fridge. I turned and limped into the shop.

"Gup! Call 9-1-1!" I yelled at the large man, then I grabbed the wooden pole out from under the tank handles lining the back wall.

I was just pulling the last of it out when he charged me from behind, knocking me to the ground. I rolled to the side, wincing as fire roared through my burned thighs. *Get up!* I grabbed the wooden shaft, hoisted myself up, and turned to face him with the pole gripped in my hands like a sword.

He snickered at me, and I jabbed at him with the broken edge of the pole, realizing my mistake in motion. He was bigger, faster, stronger. *Crap.* He easily moved aside, grabbed the stick in both hands and pulled me in. I let go and sidled toward the grocery aisle. *Nick! He doesn't have Nick!* Elation fueled me as I picked up a twenty-eight-ounce can of stewed tomatoes and threw it at his head. He yelped when it hit. I threw soup cans next, walking backward toward the camping section.

He ducked behind the shelving unit, and I turned around and pulled a camp ax off the peg board. The handle was rough, definitely an older model. I held it up in both hands and steadied myself on the balls of my feet. My right arm was bleeding through the fresh bandage. Acid pain marched up and down my body. I shivered and tightened my grip on the splintered wood. *Where are you, Bhatt?*

The shelving unit shuddered, then fell down in front of me. I stared at the dark shape rushing toward me. I raised up the ax and held menacingly.

He stopped short, three feet away, half snarling, half laughing.

Still, I kept my stance strong. I thought of all the people he had killed, bits and pieces of crime scenes floating in a disjointed river of gore. *Get behind me, Satan!* The prayer rose up unbidden, strengthening my reserve. I smiled, then I charged him.

I drove the ax down hard, blade side out, and thwacked him in the side with all my might. Instead of making contact with a pliable set of ribs, the blade hit something hard, glancing off, reverberating up through my rigid arms. Burdock turned quickly, slugging me in my bandaged ear with a fist and grabbing me by the bleeding arm. He squeezed my burned arm until I released my grip on the ax. Blinding pain thrummed through me. I couldn't breathe, couldn't see, couldn't hear.

His arms were a steel band cinching me by the waist to him. He crammed himself up against the back of my body and grunted. Sickening sensations overcame me. My adrenaline seeped away, and I wanted to cry. Shame and terror swirled within.

Burdock leaned his head into mine and uttered a deep, guttural laugh. He had me pinned up against the pegboard wall, dull edge of the ax pressed into my throat. I glanced down at his hands. He was wearing Nick's black leather gloves. "What a nice surprise, Chief. I love a dull blade. You will too. Takes a little while longer to saw through your glorious neck, but gives me more time to thoroughly enjoy you." He pressed himself against me and laughed.

Then he started sawing the rusty blade, back and forth, into my neck. I tried to move a leg, maybe stomp on his foot, but my squirming only turned him on. He sawed harder, breathed heavier. And snarled. "Is it as good for you as it is for me?"

I shut my eyes tight. *This is it. I'm really going to die.*

CHAPTER TWENTY-EIGHT

Images of Samantha, glorious and happy, arms wrapped around my mother, comforted me. She was going to be alright. She was in God's hands. A movie of all my favorite people started rolling in my mind.

I was in two places at once. The killer was present in my mind's eye but from a distance. I had floated to the corner of the bait shop's ceiling, and I watched two shows from above. Me, serene-faced, in front of a horrible man doing horrible things to me, to my body. And my life, redeemed, rolled out in love as if created, connected, shaped into one glorious strand by Someone who loved me ... and had loved me from the beginning of time.

As I watched the pictures of my life roll on, I saw behind them a meaning and a purpose. I saw even this one terrible frame—this monster sawing a rusty blade against my neck— even this was just one snapshot of an otherwise glorious life. And it didn't matter.

No one frame really matters all that much. There was a purpose far grander than any one of these frames and a Creator far more wonderful than I'd ever imagined. And He loved me. And He had a plan for me. And He wasn't shaken by my present circumstance.

A verse from Luke I'd once read played like a symphony through my mind. *Do not be afraid of those who kill the body and after that have no more that they can do.* A smile radiated through me from the inside out, His tranquility wrapping sweet arms around my spirit, mind, and body.

The smile grew. I was struck by the absurdity of the madman in front of me, and for no reason at all, I started laughing. It didn't matter. Ax or no ax, this man had no power over me. My life, my death, my everything was held only in God's hands. He was bigger than my crisis, bigger than my bondage, bigger than the slayer at my neck. Profound gratitude blossomed up within me, spreading through my limbs, easing away my pain, filling me with the sweetest peace.

The man sawing at my neck had stopped. He said something vile, but I ignored him. He pressed the blade against my bruised and bloodied throat again, but I couldn't feel it. I lifted my head to the heavens, smiled, and lovely music filled my mind. Songs of praise to the One Most High. My Deliverer.

Burdock was shouting now, saying horrid things, but I didn't care. Safe in my Savior's arms, I kept on singing praises in my soul.

A popping sound like a bottle rocket launching brushed against my ear. Burdock lurched into my body, off balance, knocking me down. Warmth splattered my face. Another pop whistled by, and he fell beside me. I turned around, stunned to discover him at my feet, two neat holes in the center of his left temple. Most of the right side of his face was … gone.

I looked up. A slender figure strode down the aisle, body set in defiant determination, followed by the man I saw in my dreams and in my arms, a high-powered rifle held light as a prayer in his arms. For the second time, I lifted my head to the sky … and laughed.

Bhatt stood aside to make room for Nick when she got to me. His eyes were shiny with tears as he handed the rifle to Bhatt.

My heart skipped. "N-Nick …" My mouth could not convey my thoughts, my voice coming out in a strangled rasp.

210

His nostrils flared as he knelt beside me, eagle eyes assessing my wounds. "Jo, my Jo …" He kissed the top of my head.

I squeezed my eyes shut. "It's okay, I'm okay …"

Nick made soothing noises as he tenderly wiped away the blood and field dressed my neck. He wrapped his arms around me, and the moment I was safely encircled by only him, I started to cry.

Nick held me, waiting for the storm to pass. "Jo, my Josie."

I wriggled against him, sniffling. "It's fine Nick. We're fine." Gup coughed, and I looked over at him, noticing for the first time he looked like an older version of Nick. Tears threatened to spill over again. I swallowed. "We're all fine."

Bhatt extended her hand to help me up as I eased away from Nick's warmth.

She put her hand up. "You are a warrior, and your man is a better shot than me. A match like this can only be made in the heavens."

I grunted up at her as I rose, every inch of my body protesting the movement, Nick's arm still half around my waist.

She sighed, eyes roving the knocked-over shelves, the pole, and the ax wet with my blood, inches from Burdock's right hand. She glanced down at him. His flannel shirt had flipped up when he fell, exposing the edge of a Kevlar vest peeking from underneath the shirt. That explained a lot.

Her eyes came to rest on Guppy staring silently at the three of us. From the looks of him, he hadn't moved a muscle since the moment I'd walked into the store.

"I never see'd him before he come into my store today. Not ten minutes before you did." Guppy left his chair and joined us to stare intently at the dead man.

"Must've been an interesting ten minutes." Memories of Gup's unusual behavior sprang up in my mind. "What made you decide to warn me off? What happened before I walked in?"

"Nothin'. I just didn't like his way. And then I had one of my feelings." He eyed me carefully. "You know."

And I did know. Gup was one of the good ones. Rough and tumble as they come—but certainly one of the good ones.

"And when you was walking in, I had a premonition." Gup looked up at me, with sober, knowing eyes. "And I didn't want you anywhere near him, nor him to even know you was here."

The first time I ever met Gup, when I was a teenager, he prayed for me. I'd made the mistake of stopping at this out-of-the-way bait shop, thinking I'd bamboozle the owner. Instead of illegally purchasing beer as I'd intended, I came away with stories of the crazy old man talking about God and praying right in front of me. Gup was definitely a praying man.

I tuned back into what he was saying. "And something come over me, like a vice grip, and I couldn't move. But I could pray."

I nodded, thinking of my own experience in his shop today—the hymn, the protection, the utter assurance of God's presence.

Nick's soft tones uttered thanks in an unsteady voice. I rested my arm on his, reveling in the feel of him by my side.

I looked back at Guppy. "Thanks, Gup." It was a poor tribute to pay to the man who'd prayed me back to life. Was he an angel? In overalls?

Guppy's eyes were soft. "Did he hurt you bad, Chief?" His eyes were awash with tears.

"Don't start, Gup." *Great.* Now I was misting up again. I walked over to him and kissed him on the cheek. "Your prayers saved my life." My voice was thick as I wrapped my arms around the weathered old man of God.

"Leave your thanks at the foot of the cross. And at the feet of your fiancé. I only did what I was told."

Nick's arm tightened around my waist.

Bhatt stood by, watching our exchange. "You rednecks are surely birds of a feather." She enunciated her words like a charm-school grad.

Guppy offered her his arm. "Relax, Officer. You'll be one of us before you know it. Why don't you come sit with me 'til the reinforcements come to clean up after you and Miss Chief? He ain't goin' nowhere. Let these kids have a moment alone."

His eyes trailed back to Burdock. "Our friends here have pressing business." He looked at Nick and me, amusement dancing across his lined face. He said this matter-of-factly like I had a scheduled event.

I wrinkled my nose, gratefully accepting a hand towel he retrieved from the floor where the grocery section used to be. "What are you talking about?" I patted my neck with the towel, and the cloth came away bloody. It didn't really hurt all that much. The skin was broken and bruised, bleeding through Nick's bandage, but not much else. Something about the prayers of a righteous man flitted through my tired mind.

Gup gave Nick an appraising look, crooking his thumb toward the door. "Ain't ya gonna get your lady outta here? Thinkin' she's seen enough of my store today."

I looked from Gup to Bhatt, steadying myself against Nick. "You wait here with the dead guy 'til the rest of the cavalry arrives," I instructed. "We'll go catch some fresh air."

Guppy nodded. "That'll work."

"As you wish." Bhatt winked at us before we turned toward the door and wandered out into the sunlight.

CHAPTER TWENTY-NINE

Nick guided me to the top of the stairs, tucking me into a seated position on the porch steps. He walked down three steps and turned to face me, every muscle in his glorious body tensing as he assessed my wounds. His jaw clenched.

"Nick, I'm okay." Warmth thickened my throat.

He ran his hand down the side of my cheek, and I let his beautiful brown eyes draw me in. Sensations ricocheted through me. My body was melting from the inside out, turning into a velvety, chocolate-fudge cake—impossibly warm and soft in his presence. *Nick.*

"How did you get here?" Sunlight glinting off glass drew my gaze to the parking area, where Gino's Z28 sat next to Bhatt's sleek red machine like horses tethered in front of a saloon, announcing the presence of lawmen.

Nick turned his head. "Gino rolled up at the next put-in a few miles up the road just as Quinn and I were pulling our kayaks onto the bank."

"How—?" Gino had built a career out of tracking men and women who didn't want to be found. Finding Nick and Quinn on the Wisconsin River was child's play for him. I nodded at Nick. "He sent you back with Bhatt?"

"I sent myself. I had to know that you were okay." His soft eyes called to me.

"Nick." I held him. I thought of how afraid I'd been for his safety, and I held on tighter.

Swaying branches off to the side of the old building caught my attention. My Cuban guardian angel, dressed completely in black, strode toward us, eyes glistening. Nick turned around at the sound of his footsteps on gravel, clasped arms with Gino then stood aside. Gino swooped in and sat next to me, setting a black case with a red cross next to him on the steps.

"I was at the trailhead, waiting for Tom to come out of the river when I heard the shot. I left Tom behind and got here as quickly as I could." Gino's eyes were glistening as he turned to meet my gaze. "Lisa stores her beloved Heckler & Koch PSG1 in the trunk of her car. That woman is an amazing shooter. I've just spoken to both Agent Dixon and the county sheriff. They are sending crime-scene techs now."

I'd seen the rifle in Nick's hands, seen the look in his eye. I knew I had. Did it matter who'd fired the fatal shot?

I placed a shaking hand on Gino's red do-rag. "I'm fine. Really. And your prayers, with Guppy's, mattered more than bullets." How to describe what I'd just experienced? "I ... G, uh ..." I shook my head.

He grabbed the railing and rose to his feet in one smooth motion. He looked at me, dark eyes flashing. Black-ops Gino took over, tenderly examining my neck. "Your neck—is it very painful? The paramedics are on their way. In the meantime ..."

His hands were gentle as he peeled off Nick's makeshift bandage, cleaned my wound, dabbed it with ointment, and applied a thick, white adhesive wrap. "This should hold you until you reach the hospital. *Mija*—this is as close as I've ever come to losing you ... this week. And I have learned that I simply could not bear it." He took my hand in his own, tears spilling over his cheeks as he softly kissed the back of my hand.

The low voices of Bhatt and Nick, reviewing what may have happened from inside the bait shop, wafted over to us. Metallic sounds of shelving units dinging together as the men picked their way over the detritus mixed with recognizable words. The stillness of the air amplified their voices.

"I got it, Bhatt." Nick's voice sounded exhausted, almost foreign.

"Thanks, Nick. But I think I know how to process a crime scene." Bhatt's response was clipped. I'd barely noticed Bhatt, I'd been so intent on Nick. Was she hurt? Worried about me? Or had something else happened?

Gino looked at me. "Stay here, *mija*. Wait quietly, rest. The ambulance will be here soon. All is well with everyone else." He rolled his eyes in the direction of the store. "I will check on them for you."

I nodded my head. "Thanks. What about Quinn?"

"He's getting picked up right about now. Relax, both of your boys are present and accounted for, *mija*." Gino smiled down at me and headed into the store.

Quinn had been one of my best childhood friends—ours was a bond that endured. The love of the same land united us in a way that couldn't be explained. We loved the same woods. We were both smitten with the way the sun broke through over Devil's Lake in the morning and the way she set in the evening.

Quinn and I once lived for nothing more than the early morning sound of a fawn crashing through the woods, looking for its mother. We were both in love with the memories we shared, with life itself, and with the land of our youth.

But the love I had for my Nick Vitarello eclipsed my love of the land.

I stood up, intending to limp after Gino and stopped. Pain sliced through me with every step.

Gino must've heard me grunting. He appeared next to me, glowering. "Why are you on your feet?"

"I'm fine. I'm fine." I tried to swat him away as he moved in, deftly maneuvering my shoulder over his, careful to avoid my bandages, transferring my weight to his. "Ooh, that is better actually. You may proceed."

He nodded and instead of moving ahead, he swooped down and gathered me into his arms, carrying me like a toddler off the porch, into the parking lot. He kept walking, away from the store, toward the tree line. Gino carried me to a huge tree stump, lowering me gently onto its sturdy seat. I panted for a moment, grateful to be motionless, waiting for the pounding in my head to fade to a manageable thrum. I sucked in a deep breath and let it out slowly before training my eyes on the bait shop.

Gino stood beside me as first Nick, then Bhatt scrambled out of the store and stood still at the sight of us, at the sight of *me*. Bhatt's eyes grew wide as saucers when she saw me sitting alone. She nodded at Gino, elbowed Nick in the ribs and retreated into the store.

Nick stood alone, waning sunlight framing his body, still as a buck.

"Go to your woman, man." Gino walked toward the store, nodding as he passed Nick.

I sat transfixed, my body yearning for Nick's. A clarion call as ancient as time was welling up from deep within. Had he heard it? Would he answer me?

Nick's body softened into motion, and he kept his eyes locked on mine as he picked his way through the gravel, mud, and roots on his way to me. I wanted to stand up, but exhaustion and a host of stronger feelings kept me pinned to the trunk. Out of the corner of my eye, I could see Bhatt lock arms with Gino on the bait shop porch, shifting her weight while she watched Nick swing around and sit down next to me.

Nick's breathing slowed as he sat next to me on the aged stump. As Gino followed Bhatt back inside, we eased closer until every inch of our bodies that could touch moved together. His damp jacket felt cool against my skin.

I tugged at the thick leather. "You didn't think to shed this thing before going overboard?"

He smiled. "No. I know how much you like it." He kissed the top of my head, his hands moving carefully to my face. "Look what he did to you." He drew back, examining me.

"Relax, baby—we've been over this. I'm fine." I took his hands away from the bandage on my neck and placed them around my waist.

He yielded to my touch, leaning his head toward me, drawing his lips near enough to kiss. I pulled the collar of his wet leather jacket down and nuzzled his neck, breathing in the scent of him.

The touch of my lips against his collarbone unleashed a torrent inside me. An overpowering wall of impossibly tough love cascaded over me, and my heart opened to receive him. I pushed my hands against the stump and struggled to my feet, careful to keep his hands around my waist. My lips traced his brow, leaving soft kisses in their wake. I kissed his eyelids, drawing my fingertips across his sculpted cheekbones. *My Italian god.* An electric verse from Exodus 20 sparked through my mind. *I am the Lord Your God ... You shall have no other gods before Me.*

I stand corrected.

I meant, my Italian hottie. You *are my God, heavenly Father.*

I opened my eyes. Nick was staring at me intently, soft brown eyes shining with love. It was now or never.

"So, Nick, uh ..."

His eyes twinkled, but he said nothing.

"Well, what I'm trying to say is ..." It was all so clear in my heart, in my head. *Why can't I find the right words?*

"Yes?" Nick drew the word out, his voice laced with mischief.

"So, it, uh … well, it's more of a … you know, I mean, it's like … What I'm trying to say is …"

"Maybe I can help." Nick leaned back and took a deep breath. Easing himself off the stump, he slipped to his knees.

He took my hands in his. "Josephine Oliver. I have something to say to you. From the moment we met—"

"Are you cold? I feel cold. And you're soaking wet. Isn't it chilly out here?" I willed myself to stop talking. I hoped my nerves would get the memo. *Soon.*

He smiled. "From the first day I saw you, all hot and sassy in your brand-new badge, barking out orders at resentful recruits—"

I squeezed his hands and smiled. "Like you?"

"From that moment forward, and through all the moments in between that have brought us to right now, you've become the best part of my life. My North Star."

Embers of delight warmed me from somewhere deep inside.

"I realized years ago that you're family. And then one day I knew …"

Clouds cleared from a fall sky in my mind. Butterflies fluttered in my stomach. "Oh, Nick …"

"I'm in love with you. And the only other woman I love almost as much is a tough little girl. And I want nothing more than for you, and me, and Sammie …" He shifted on the ground, popping one knee up.

Time slowed to a crawl, and the breeze moved through the trees, leaf by leaf. Stars burst in my head as his hand disappeared into an inner pocket of his leather jacket. *The jacket. He'd kept the jacket at all costs today.* He took my left hand and kissed it. Then he held up an impossibly beautiful diamond ring.

"Josie, marry me. Please."

I lifted my hand, stretching it out to him. Tears welled up as he nudged the ring onto my finger. "Yes, Nick. Yes." I joined him on the ground, running my hands over his face, looking into his deep brown eyes. My heart swelled up, heat flushed my face.

He opened his jacket a second time, unzipping an inner compartment and withdrawing a sheaf of papers, wrapped tightly in plastic.

I gasped. "Nick, is that?"

"Shhh." He traced his finger over my lips, kissed me, then tugged the papers from the bag and unfolded them.

The gold seal of the Paradise County Courthouse was the first thing I saw. Right next to the signature of the judge who had finally set my daughter free. To be my daughter. "Nick. We're going to have a baby. A beautiful seven-year-old girl." I smiled, joy blossoming through me as I snuggled into his chest.

Nick's arms tightened around me. "Even better. We already have her." He kissed the top of my head and held me close. Dusk had blanketed the clearing, last gasps of steam rising off the river as temperatures collided over the roiling water. I looked up at the darkening sky, Nick's anchoring presence releasing the tight-muscled, clenched-gut feeling I spent too much of my waking hours caught up in. I stayed present, linked with him, watching the sky move from golds and pinks to a deep blue, glittering with nascent stars.

From the safety of Nick's arms, I drifted. Jagged photos of the people I've loved and lost popped up in my mind's eye, then toppled like targets at a shooting gallery. Del and me, deliriously happy—replaced by me alone, bruised, sobbing. Del and his mistress on our boat at our house—replaced by that final horrible picture of them forever etched in my memory. Sammie, war-torn and weary eyed—replaced by Sammie, glowing and safely wrapped up between Nick and me.

The garish shooting gallery faded away and softened images fell gently like oak leaves on a fall day. Gino's soft brown eyes, shining with love. Cliff and Georgi, sitting on their back porch. Mitch, Jules, and my women and men in blue standing together back in Haversport. The images fell faster in my mind, covering a forest floor, ready for harvest. Each photo stood alone, yet connected. My neighbors, Jim and Donna, dogs frolicking at their feet, stood alone, yet rooted together with all of the other people woven into my life. My simple, beautiful life, grounded in community.

I pressed my ear against Nick's chest, reveling in the heartbeat of the man I loved—solid, steady, and always right there in front of me. Delight surged through me. *This is the man I want. The love I need. The perfect father for my Sammie.*

I closed my eyes and breathed a prayer of thanks. God had brought this amazing man into my life again and again and again. Nick Vitarello was my man. Had always been my man, would always be my man. That it'd taken me at least two near-death experiences and one bad marriage to realize he was meant for me only served to underscore the truth. Nick was mine, and I was his.

God had answered my wandering heart's cry for love—for an anchor for my heart, just as He was the anchor for my soul.

ABOUT THE AUTHOR

Catherine Finger loves to dream, write, and tell stories. Recently retired from a wonderful career in public education, she celebrates the ability to choose how to spend her time in a new way during the second half of life. So far, she chooses to write books, ride horses, serve others, and generally find her way into and out of trouble both on the road and at home. She lives in the Midwest with a warm and wonderful combination of family and friends.

Catherine loves to interact with her readers at www. CatherineFinger.com. Follow her on Facebook at Catherine Finger, Author and on Twitter at Catherine Finger@ BeJoOliver.

Made in the USA
Lexington, KY
16 June 2017